T0151409

Cha-Ching!

Cha-Ching!

Ali Liebegott

CITY LIGHTS
SisterSpit

San Francisco

Cover photo by Sara Seinberg

Acknowledgments
Thank you to the following for your various forms of support during the
writing of this book: my family, Lucy Corin, Christina Frank, Pawsitive
Tails, RADAR Productions & The RADAR Lab, Rainbow Grocery Co-
Operative, Nikki Simms, Erin Conley, Cassie J. Sneider, Sarah Fran Wisby,
and everyone at City Lights/Sister Spit Books.

Also, a deep gratitude goes to Beth Pickens for love, support, and editing
help and Michelle Tea, for two decades of literary friendship.

Lastly, to Elaine Katzenberger for your expert editing skills. I'm eternally
grateful.

Library of Congress Cataloging-in-Publication Data
Liebegott, Ali.
  Cha-ching! / Ali Liebegott.
     pages cm
  ISBN 978-0-87286-570-9
  1. Lesbians—Fiction. 2. Self-realization in women—Fiction. I. Title.

PS3612.I327C48 2013
813'.6--dc23

                         2012046896

City Lights Books are published at the City Lights Bookstore
261 Columbus Avenue
San Francisco, CA 94133
www.citylights.com

"A novel is never anything, but a philosophy put into images." —*Albert Camus*

for famig and other famig

one

It was 1994, the year of bad, low-blood-sugar decisions. As soon as Theo was done watching her favorite episode of *Top 25 Best 911 Emergencies* she planned to leave her empty San Francisco apartment and move to New York. She sat on the cold hardwood floor and absorbed the grave situation of a man who'd become trapped in the bottom of a garbage truck. A passerby had called 911 after hearing what sounded like "human cries" coming from the truck.

Local police were instructed to pull over every garbage truck in a three-mile radius of where the man had reported the cries. When the right one was finally found, a policeman stood at the rear of the truck and spoke clearly into his megaphone, "Is anyone in there? Can you hear me?" while two sanitation workers in bright orange vests snickered in the background, smoking cigarettes.

The second time the policeman called into the garbage truck a tiny muffled voice said, "Yes, sir. I'm down here."

This was Theo's favorite episode because the TV show never discussed how a person might find himself trapped in the bottom of a garbage truck. She knew there were only a few explanations: mental illness, drunkenness, homelessness, or a combination of the three, but by not exploring any of the options the TV show was saying, "Don't judge! We're all five decisions away from waking up in the bottom of a garbage truck." And when the man was pulled gently by his arms from piles of oozing plastic bags, the TV show did him the additional honor of digitally blurring his face to protect his anonymity.

She snapped off the small black-and-white TV but remained seated in front of it until the last bit of light fizzled into the center of the screen like a dying star. Then she yanked the thick black cord from the wall. She wasn't moving this piece of shit all the way across the country. It was warm in her arms when she picked it up to carry it to the community free box. Theo climbed the two flights of stairs and opened the door that led to the roof. The cold San Francisco wind hit her squarely in the face. When she was sure she could steal no more warmth from the TV she set it down on the seat of a discarded gray office chair. There was almost never anything good in the free box, yet Theo looked at the pile daily when she passed it on her way to smoke. With the exception of her TV it held the same things as yesterday: the office chair, some shitty glass picture frames, rock-climbing shoes, and a broken, beige-carpeted cat tree. All of it was trash, really, but people often left trash in the free box when it wouldn't fit in the trash can or they didn't want to walk the extra paces to the garbage chute.

In New York Theo would be a person who didn't drink or smoke or watch TV. She'd transform herself into a well-read adult, starting with the complete works of Fyodor Dostoyevsky, then move her way through biographies of famous painters. She'd always wanted to take a painting class and find out if she was secretly a brilliant artist. In New York, she'd get a gym membership—she could read *Crime and Punishment* on the stationary bicycle. Before she turned thirty she wanted to be able to go to a party and have a conversation that involved *anything* besides details from true-crime shows.

Theo lived in a large white apartment building across from some housing projects that were painted a terrible baby-shit brown. When she first moved into the neighborhood, she didn't want to be like the people who went out of their way to walk on the opposite side of the street, but the regular group of boys on the corner who taunted and shouted and sometimes threw empty beer bottles at people's heads had quickly weakened her resolve. When she saw them outside, she learned to cross the street, look the other way, become very involved in lighting her cigarette.

Two weeks after moving into her apartment, the police cracked a pit bull ring in the projects. A swarm of cop cars screeched to a halt in the intersection, flung their doors open and kept their red and blue lights swirling as they ran in and busted the operation. The dogcatcher was a long-haired Latina butch named Denise who Theo knew from the bars. Denise did an intricate dance, pushing a ten-foot pole with a loop at the end toward each dog. She was like a lifeguard at a city pool inserting the pole into the water for the drowning swimmer, but to be saved the dogs needed to be calm and put their paws over the wire loop. And to be calm they needed to have had entirely different paths up until this point in their lives, needed to have grown up from puppyhood not being stabbed in the ribs with screwdrivers for the sole purpose of making them mean.

Denise herded the beautiful, unsaveable dogs one at a time out of the projects and into the convoy of white Animal Care and Control vans. They looked like old-fashioned baseball catchers with wire muzzles strapped over their jaws. Theo knew they would be euthanized as she watched them, one at a time, lunge at Denise, even while muzzled.

Theo had watched the entire scene while peeking out from behind the mini-blinds of her bedroom window. Her bedroom window was not unlike her small black-and-white TV in that it only got reception to a few stations. When Theo woke at 7 AM, she pulled her blinds up a few inches to turn on Taco Lady TV. The Taco Lady would have already arrived two hours ago in her pickup and speedily set up her mobile food cart, stretching a large, bright blue plastic tarp over the truck's rooftop and snapping two strong poles into place to create a little awning. She'd plugged a silver percolator into a generator and arranged a tall stack of Styrofoam cups to sell coffee to people walking to the bus stop. Even though there were "nice" cafes five blocks away, Theo was not willing to pay three dollars for a cup of coffee, nor did she want to sit next to people who wore two-hundred-dollar jeans. Instead, she shuffled across the street and for a single dollar purchased an enormous coffee and a dry Mexican pastry. It was like having a cameo appearance on the television show she was watching. Then she'd return to her apartment, sit down on her bed, and drink her coffee while watching the rest of Taco Lady TV. Many people shuffled over to the Taco Lady's truck for their morning provisions. Not everyone got a pastry. Some left with a tostada, slightly larger than the tiny white paper plate it was served on. When Theo walked to her job as a cashier at the Party Store she found those tiny plates in the gutter as far as ten blocks away. The plethora of discarded plates were the Taco Lady's own soaring stock index. Every day but Sunday the Taco Lady worked from 5 AM till midnight, opening a variety of coolers from the back of her truck to prepare tacos and tortas for the neighborhood. Theo often found herself worrying that the Taco Lady was not getting enough sleep.

On days that Theo was extra sensitive and the boys on the corner extra rambunctious, instead of leaving the house for something to eat she would try to go to sleep early, a trick she'd learned from reading Depression-era books about poor parents trying to distract the kids from their hunger. It rarely worked; often she just tossed and turned with a terrible hunger headache.

The Taco Lady had to put up with the boys' antics, too.

"Oh, you want me to pay? I thought it was free," they said to her.

The Taco Lady would face them down stoically, wordlessly, until they fell into a quiet respect and paid.

Around noon, if Theo wasn't at work she'd change the channel from Taco Lady TV to Thug TV and start watching the boys on the corner shout at girls or fuck with each other or smoke a blunt, and late at night when she was sleeping, she'd be awoken by Screeching Tire TV. Some of those same boys would get into their classic cars and start doing donuts in the intersection until everything was obscured by the smoke of burning tires on pavement. The first time Theo had raised her blinds in the middle of the night and seen the smoke she'd panicked, wondering if there was a fire.

But today was the last day she would have to deal with those boys on the corner.

She lit what she hoped would be the last cigarette of her life and paced the perimeter of the roof, taking in the dome of City Hall. A few faint stars hovered shyly above the lights outlining the Bay Bridge, and Theo tried to make herself feel some emotion about leaving the city she'd lived in for ten years, but she felt only cold and hungover. Theo often compared her own lack of emotions to the kind displayed by characters in movies. If she were a character in a movie she'd get teary looking at City Hall, or have an epiphany about moving all the way across the country. At the very least she'd feel the devastating, crushing blow of knowing she would never again watch a crime show on the tiny black-and-white TV.

She'd gone out of her way in life to feel nothing and maybe it had backfired, the same way getting drunk every day and learning nothing in high school had backfired. She was almost thirty and had no idea what made a moon full or what countries bordered which. Once she'd bought a shower curtain with a map of the world to make up for the high school geography classes she'd been too drunk to learn anything in. But after bragging to everyone about Italy being the boot, she'd begun to turn the other way in the shower, irritated by her lack of knowledge.

Her lip throbbed. Her friends had thrown her a going away party, a last hurrah, and she'd accidentally bitten through her lip when a friend had flung her straight off the dance floor into a cement pillar. She felt ashamed. She was too old to be having bar injuries.

"I'm not drinking in New York," she'd said, trying to get as drunk as possible to compensate for all the drunks she'd never have again.

Theo took a drag from her cigarette and hung her head over the edge of the rooftop. A green city garbage truck idled, and Theo saw the remnants of a giant supermarket sheet cake lying next to some dirty diapers. For a brief second she thought about the man from the TV show and wondered how he had survived. A breeze swept the garbage truck fumes right up into her face. She felt her stomach turn and then she retched a liquid pile of mostly gin and tonics littered with tiny pieces of undigested orange cheese.

If life could be started over any time any place, why not start over in New York, where at the very least a person could purchase a slice of pizza any hour of the day? Theo's belongings were already loaded in her truck. By the time she got to New York her hangover would be gone, her head would be clear and she would be something! An artist! An entrepreneur! An inventor! She had so many ideas: like the travel mug in the shape of a toilet, it would have a toilet seat that went down for a lid. She'd also always wanted to make a mood ring for alcoholics—the rainbow of colors could translate into words like *lonely*, and *sorry*, and *marry me*. A burst of laughter interrupted her entrepreneurial thoughts. The boys from the corner were up on the roof across the street. Her impulse was to duck down and hide but she remembered she was moving to New York as soon as she finished what was now the third of her last cigarettes and so she felt less afraid. She watched their silhouettes move and tried to decipher their indistinguishable murmurs. Their laughter sounded drug-induced. Theo watched as they walked together to the edge of the roof. She stood very still. What if they had that slingshot she'd seen them with a few weeks ago, using pigeons as target practice? What if this time they were aiming at her face?

"Now!" she heard one of the boys yell, and all four heaved a long duffel bag over the side of the roof. The bag fell fast and heavy, hitting the top of the Taco Lady's makeshift awning with a large *thwap!* Then the awning gave way, its aluminum poles splaying out slowly like the legs on a tired giraffe. The Taco Lady scurried out and bent over the duffel bag. Then she screamed twice, and Theo heard the sharp yelp of a dog.

Theo ran down the stairs, two at a time. Her whole life she'd been terrible in an emergency, paralyzed by her own fear, but this was different—*a dog's life was at stake*. When the Taco Lady saw Theo approach, she began to gesture toward the sky and Theo didn't know if she was trying to indicate God or the falling dog. Theo pushed the fear down in her stomach and knelt down next to the blue duffel bag, where she was relieved to see the dog shivering. It wasn't dead. The pit bull watched her from the corners of its eyes and Theo studied the long scar that ran down the left side of its head, like an exaggerated part in the hair of a dapper, old-fashioned movie star.

"Hello," Theo said to the dog.

The whites of the dog's giant eyes flicked over at her as it panted. She tried to send a message of trust from her heart into the dog's while assessing how she might pick it up. Should she unzip the bag and let the dog out, or carry it like a suitcase to the 24-hour vet? Theo looked over at the Taco Lady, who remained a safe distance away from any gore and then back at the dog.

"I'm not going to hurt you," she said softly, reaching out to smooth the fur on the dog's head.

It let out a high shriek as Theo's hand approached.

"Okay," she told the dog and then motioned to the Taco Lady, who remained frozen.

"Ayúdame, por favor," Theo asked, holding one handle of the duffel bag out for the Taco Lady to grab.

She came over reluctantly, and together they lifted the dog. There was a smear of blood on the tarp where the dog had landed, and Theo felt a wave of panic go through her.

"I'm going to take it to the vet," she said slowly.

"Veterinario?" the Taco Lady asked.

"Sí."

The Taco Lady nodded, and they lifted the dog and carried it to Theo's truck, carefully setting it onto the passenger's seat.

The entire drive to the vet, Theo watched to make sure the dog was breathing and its eyes were open. She double parked when she arrived, leaving the dog on the passenger seat, still zipped in the duffel bag, and ran inside to tell the receptionist what had happened. Two young women in scrubs immediately ran to the truck and removed the dog, placing it on a stretcher and carrying it inside.

"As soon as we know how serious this is, Dr. West will come get you," the receptionist said. "In the meantime, have a cup of coffee."

So Theo poured a cup of complimentary coffee and took a seat in the empty waiting room. She was exhausted and the day had just started. Every time she heard a door open she craned her head around looking for some news of the dog. After three cups of coffee and a trashy Hollywood magazine, a young, dark-skinned black woman in a white lab coat came into the waiting room and sat down next to Theo.

"I'm Dr. West," the woman said.

"Hello," Theo said.

"That is one unbelievably lucky dog," Dr. West said smiling. "Besides a few stitches, she only has a broken right front leg."

"Oh, God," Theo said.

"She was unbelievably lucky," Dr. West repeated.

"I bet it was the tarp," Theo said.

Dr. West looked at her.

"When they threw her off the roof she landed on the Taco Lady's tarp—her little awning."

Theo then briefly recounted the story of the boys and the pit bull ring to Dr. West, who listened in horror and then said, "So you don't know whose dog it is?"

"I think it was their dog," Theo said. "Because of the scar on its head. Maybe it was a fighting dog."

Dr. West nodded.

"I don't really know. I'm supposed to be moving to New York today," Theo said.

"Oh."

"I was on the roof smoking a cigarette, and then all this happened."

"Well, we sedated her a little to calm her down so we can put the cast on. Do you want to get a cup of coffee and come back in an hour and we'll go from there?"

"Okay."

"Maybe you're supposed to have a dog in New York," Dr. West said, smiling.

Whenever Theo saw people her own age with careers she wondered how they'd already amounted to something. Did they come from good families? How had they known which of their dreams was trustworthy enough to follow? Theo was afraid to pour any more coffee into her queasy stomach and decided to walk to the corner store for cigarettes and a pack of crumb donuts.

"Good morning," she said to the cashier, "Can I get a pack of those?" putting the crumb donuts on the counter and pointing to the Lucky Strikes.

The cashier rang her up silently, looking at her suspiciously. Then Theo realized he was staring at her T-shirt covered in bloodstains as if she was some kind of criminal.

"I just saved a dog's life," she told him indignantly, thinking he would put two and two together since the emergency vet was across the street, but he looked at her with disgust.

The bloodstains were actually from her bar injury the night before, when she bit through her lip on the dance floor, but she didn't feel bad lying to the asshole cashier. She lit a cigarette and walked to her truck. Halfway through it she remembered she was quitting. Fuck it, Theo thought. She was celebrating the dog's blind luck.

A few years back Theo had read a newspaper article about a math teacher who got caught in the crossfire of a gang fight. She'd cut out the story and pasted it to her refrigerator: "What Are the Odds: Statistician's Life Saved When Bullet Becomes Lodged in the Window of his Scientific Calculator." Without the calculator in his breast pocket the bullet would have pierced his heart. The teacher posed in the newspaper photo holding up the calculator that had saved his life, the bullet mounted in it like a tiny taxidermied deer head. These kind of stories gave Theo hope that for every hundred cruel things the universe could throw around, occasionally blind luck prevailed.

After she finished her cigarette she got in the truck and ate the entire pack of mini donuts in less than a minute. Her head and body ached. She needed a shower and a good night's sleep, and maybe twelve gallons of water to clear out her system. She pulled a clean T-shirt out the bag of necessities she'd packed for the drive to New York, and changed out of her bloodstained version.

She thought about what Dr. West had said: *Maybe you're supposed to have a dog in New York.* She laid the bloody shirt down on the passenger seat like a blanket and then she rummaged around in her bag for her toothbrush. She came across the wig her neighbor Olivia had given her for the solo cross-country drive.

"So you're not murdered in a creepy rest stop," Olivia had said flatly.

Olivia had moved to San Francisco from Ohio, driving across country and negotiating public restrooms as a trans-woman who didn't always pass as female. She knew Theo would be in the same predicament, because even in San Francisco, people often didn't know what the fuck to make of Theo. When she'd first moved into her apartment building and hadn't yet lost the courage to walk by the boys on the corner, they'd yell, "What the fuck are you?" "What the fuck are you" can be translated into a variety of languages. *Sir? Ma'am? Sir? Señor? Señora? Monsieur? Madame?* She and Olivia joked that she was "the sirma'amsir"—like some kind of elusive two-toed sloth that lazed about the rainforest floor. They imagined the nature documentary, with the sound of twigs breaking and leaves moving and then a strong British accent whispering, "The timid sirma'amsir can be seen here hiding in the thick foliage, drinking Coca-Cola and chain-smoking."

The problem wasn't being mistaken for a man, it was in that second later, when she was discovered to be female. The variety of responses was plentiful. Some people became angry, thinking she was purposely trying to mislead them about her gender, others so embarrassed that they tried to deflect their embarrassment by sharing ridiculous anecdotes, like how they'd once been mistaken for a little boy in the church bathroom when they were eight years old. It was best when everyone just pretended nothing was amiss and Theo could continue with her business at hand: ordering a hamburger, buying stamps, or getting a seven-dollar haircut.

Theo spent a lot of time with Olivia since they were both homebodies who lived across the hall from each other. Olivia had kept Theo steady company during the last week as she packed and cleaned her apartment. They took a break one day because Olivia wanted to go to the wig shop. Theo had never been to a wig shop before, and she milled about assessing the hairstyles on the assortment of Styrofoam heads until she found one that came closest to the hair she'd had her senior year in high school. It was long, down to the middle of her back, wavy, and light brown. She put it on.

"What do you think?" she asked, turning to Olivia who was trying on a dark red wig with blonde highlights.

"Mousy."

Theo felt a little hurt and wanted to tell Olivia the wig she was looking at was too young for someone in her mid-forties.

"What about mine?" she asked.

"Divorcée," Theo replied.

They both ignored each other on the drive back. The next day Olivia knocked on Theo's door and invited her over for drinks. Theo loved how Olivia's apartment felt like a historical site, with its fainting couch and old Victrola. She decided to bring her some roses. Their friendship had always been platonic, but a few times when they'd been drinking, Theo had felt like they were on the verge of having an affair.

"I'm sorry I said you looked like a divorcée," Theo said, handing Olivia the roses.

"Well, I'm not sorry I said you looked mousy. Friends tell each other the truth."

Olivia walked over to the Victrola and dropped on a big band record.

Crackers, Olivia's white cat, was sleeping on the shelf

with the records. Her fur was saturated with secondhand smoke because Olivia never opened her windows. The first time Theo had tried to hug the cat, the smell of its fur almost made her throw it across the room.

Theo sat down at Olivia's vanity while she waited for her friend to return with the drinks. She fiddled with a pair of clip-on bangs. Stuck between the mirror and vanity frame was a strip of photo booth pictures they'd taken one night after getting blotto at the bar. Olivia was wearing the clip-on bangs and giant, black sunglasses. She held her martini glass up at four different angles as if to say, *Cheers*. Theo looked virtually the same in each shot, staring straight ahead with dark circles under her eyes, with her Marine-style haircut and torn hooded sweatshirt. She gave the camera the finger, while keeping her other arm slung around Olivia's shoulder coolly. This was the first night Theo thought they were going to hook up. They'd snorted some speed and looked at each other a little too long, a little too close in a bathroom stall. Then the rest of the night Theo tried to get the courage up to kiss Olivia but never did.

"This is a going-away present," Olivia said, sliding a cardboard box across the floor.

Theo felt the sadness creep up inside her. Olivia was her family. She opened the box, and inside was the brown wig she'd tried on in the store.

Theo looked at her, confused.

"I thought it might be nice for driving across country," Olivia started. "You can wear it when you go into restrooms so you don't get murdered. It was either this wig or a felt moustache set. Believe me, the middle of the country won't understand you."

Theo put the wig on and turned to the mirror.

"It's really terrible," Olivia said. "I gave it to you early so we can work on it."

Theo primped in Olivia's mirror. "Do I look like a beautiful woman?" she joked.

"No, you look like a man wearing a woman's wig."

The wig was flattened on one side from where it had been packed in the box, and Olivia picked at it with her fingers, then stepped back.

Theo felt hopeful for a moment.

"I only need it for the rest stop. I'm not looking for a husband."

"Wear it every day until you leave and let it shape to your head."

After a few days of wearing it around the house while she washed the dishes Theo reported back to Olivia.

"Well?" she asked when Olivia opened the door.

"You look like that woman I saw on TV who was shot in the head and lived."

"Why did you give me a present if you're just going to make fun of me?"

"Do you know who I mean?" Olivia said, ignoring her.

Theo did. She'd read the paper about the woman caught in the middle of a robbery. Another kind of miracle, where the bullet went just the right way through her brain so that she could still talk and hold down a job. When the newspaper showed the photos of her recovery she was smiling, but the left side of her head was caved in, like Theo's wig. The doctors had taken out part of her skull to let her lucky brain swell. If you didn't know she'd been shot in the head you might think she'd fallen asleep with her head pressed into the window on a Greyhound bus that had been traveling for three hundred years.

The last thing Olivia said when she hugged Theo good-bye was, "Don't linger in the restroom and you won't scare anyone. And send me a postcard from Cleveland."

Theo scared women in public restrooms the way brooms scare stray dogs. Theo just had to come near the entrance of a ladies' room and women stopped speaking altogether, and pointed for her to walk in the other direction.

Once an old lady in a casino had grumbled, "Mujeres, mujeres."

When Theo wouldn't leave she gave one more, "Mujeres," while pointing at the toilets.

"Yo soy," Theo said, hitting her chest with her hand because she didn't know how to say she was the timid sirma'amsir searching for shelter in a diminished habitat.

⋮

When Theo woke up in her truck, she was still holding the toothbrush she'd fished out of her backpack. Several hours had passed since she was supposed to have returned for the dog, and she shoved the toothbrush in her pocket and bolted back into the vet's office.

The receptionist smiled when she saw Theo.

"Let me get Dr. West," she said.

A moment later Dr. West appeared, leading the dog on a thin, bright blue leash. Its brindled head was inside a clear lampshade and on its front right leg was a hot-pink cast. The dog swayed a little, sedated.

"Break this painkiller in half and give it to her twice a day," she said, handing Theo a prescription bottle.

Theo's mouth salivated as she held the bottle of opiates.

"The cast will need to stay on for at least a month. The stitches can come out in seven days," Dr. West continued.

It was as if Dr. West had hypnotized Theo. It was her dog, right? Fate? She'd been on the roof and seen it fall. If she didn't take it, it would probably be put down. It didn't matter; by this point Theo was too embarrassed to say, "Oh, actually I'm not taking the dog." Instead she just kept nodding and saying, "Of course."

"This whole visit is on the house," Dr. West said, "and here's a bag of dog food to start."

Theo stared at the drugged dog.

"What will you name her?"

Theo's eyes settled on the thick scar across the dog's head.

"What do you think about Cary Grant?" Theo said. "Doesn't this scar kind of look like Cary Grant's hair?"

Dr. West laughed, petting the dog's back haunches.

"Call me here if you have any questions at all," Dr. West said.

Theo took her card and the dog and the bag of dog food out to the truck, and each time the dog took a step its cast made a tiny click on the sidewalk.

"Want to go to New York?" Theo asked, setting the dog down on the bloody T-shirt that was now her blanket.

By the time she put her key into the ignition, Cary Grant was already asleep.

two

Theo wasn't taking a meandering road trip across America trying to determine her fate through the text of quirky road signs. She'd already taken that trip. Many times. She just wanted to hurry up and get to New York so she could be a new person. Her lungs hurt from chain-smoking, but she needed the cigarettes to keep her awake while she was driving and also, *Jesus Christ—she'd already quit drinking, what more was expected of a person in one lifetime?*

Cary Grant spent most of the first day curled up sleeping, her pink cast hanging over the edge of the passenger seat. The rest of the time the dog stared straight ahead, sadly, at nothing. Theo took off the lampshade, but it didn't help. At rest stops, Theo put on her Butch Bathroom Wig and tried to get the dog to pee or eat or drink something. She was sure they both looked down on their luck to passersby— Cary Grant with her cast and stitches and Theo with her wig askew and her busted lip. She noticed people at the rest stops going out of their way to avoid her, the same way she'd kept a wary distance from the boys on the corner in her old neighborhood. At one rest stop, when Theo leaned over to fill the dog's water dish, her wig slid off and landed on the sidewalk.

"Oh my God!" she heard a woman who was standing near the vending machines gasp.

Theo picked up her wig with one hand and antagonistically waved hello with the other. When the woman didn't wave back, she became enraged.

"I fucking have cancer," she yelled, jamming the wig back onto her head.

The adrenaline that comes with telling a flagrant lie rushed through her veins as she led Cary Grant back to the truck. Theo loved lying to strangers and often felt justified, telling herself they probably hated gay people. But she'd also been raised with just enough Catholicism to feel guilty—what if that woman had cancer herself? Now Theo's punishment would be to get cancer.

A few summers ago Theo had gotten a second job to save some money. She worked at the baseball stadium selling cotton candy. The majority of her coworkers were sixteen-year-old boys who'd been given the jobs in an effort to keep them out of gangs. It was some of the hardest work she'd ever done, climbing up and down the stadium stairs holding a plywood board with fifty cones of cotton candy stuck into it. After her shift, she practically crawled to the bus stop, her legs and feet hurt so badly. One day walking to the bus stop her coworker asked her if she had a boyfriend.

Theo looked at him incredulously and said, "A boyfriend?"

"Yeah," he said.

"No. I'm gaaaayyyyy," she told him. She said the word *gay* very slowly and clearly, like it was a special flower the class was learning about.

"Oh," her coworker said. "I didn't know. I just thought you had cancer."

⋮

Cary Grant was beginning to adjust to her new relationship with Theo. On the second day, she finally clicked over to the water dish and took a few timid sips. She still slept most of the day, but she also began to sit up and look out the window when the truck changed speed on the interstate. She hadn't eaten any of the kibble, so Theo bought a package of hot dogs from a truck stop and broke one into a few pieces. She held one in the palm of her hand, flush with the seat and a few inches from Cary Grant. The dog sniffed but didn't take it.

"It's okay," Theo said.

She could see the dog extend her neck forward as if she was going to take the hot dog but then retreat, and it killed Theo to see her so afraid. She tossed the piece of hot dog onto the seat near Cary Grant's paws. The dog sniffed, then swallowed it without chewing. She threw another piece, and Cary Grant gobbled that one, too. Theo felt like she might cry from joy. Cary Grant glanced at her shyly, waiting for her to throw another piece.

"Here you go," Theo said, this time trying to get the dog to take the food directly. She held the hot dog under the dog's nose and watched the very tip of Cary Grant's tail wag nervously.

"It's all for you," she said, and the dog reached forward and seized the hot dog from her hand.

"What a good girl," Theo cooed, taking in the giant scar on Cary Grant's head and all the other scars that crisscrossed her body.

The first two nights, they slept in Motel 6 parking lots trying to save money. Theo reclined her seat and Cary Grant remained shotgun, snoring lightly with her hot pink cast straight out in front of her. On the third night Theo purchased a cheap room in a small casino and dog track outside of St. Louis. She desperately needed a shower and a good night's sleep for her sore back.

She led the dog into the motel room and dumped her belongings on the bed. Then she shoved one of the dog's painkillers into a piece of hot dog and dropped it in the bowl with some kibble next to the nightstand. She flipped on the TV so the dog would have some background noise and got into the shower. The hot water felt good on her filthy body and she stayed in there long enough to feel guilty for wasting water. When she opened the bathroom door she found the dog waiting for her shyly.

"Cary Grant!" she said happily, and the dog wagged once nervously then disappeared around the corner.

Her bowl was empty; she'd finally eaten. Theo put on her pajamas and crawled under the sheets.

"Come here," she said, patting the mattress a few times, but the dog's ears went back when she did that.

"Cary Grant," Theo said quietly.

She said it a few times until she could feel some meaning behind it. The next time she patted the mattress, she did it lightly, and the dog jumped up, curling into a circle at the foot of the bed.

Theo flipped through the channels until she landed on an episode of *Hooked*. She'd seen this one before, about a woman who smoked twenty-five PCP cigarettes a day. How was there enough time in the day to smoke twenty-five PCP cigarettes? And despite smoking twenty-five PCP cigarettes a day, the woman still held down two jobs: one as a prostitute and the other as an ordained minister who married people, drive-thru-chapel style.

"I didn't like the taste of alcohol at first," the woman said, recounting how her addiction had begun with just a few beers and then escalated to twenty-five PCP cigarettes a day. "I had to force myself to like it."

A camera panned to a middle-aged white man with a moustache. The banner underneath him said, "Addiction Specialist."

"She needs help," the addiction specialist told the woman's mother.

"Well, that's a no-brainer! Right, Cary Grant?"

But the dog had fallen asleep. When I get to New York, maybe I'll be an addiction specialist too, Theo thought. She imagined herself behind a giant mahogany desk, knee-deep in losing lottery scratch-offs, chain-smoking and wearing one of those bright yellow helmets that hold two beers at a time. The sign on her desk would read, "The Addiction Specialist is IN."

Theo was simultaneously exhausted and wired. She turned off the TV and lay in the dark feeling her mind race. She had never smoked PCP, but when she was eight her mother had gotten revved up after watching something on the news, and had lectured Theo to be on guard for strangers who might offer her PCP.

"What is it?" Theo had asked.

"An elephant tranquilizer."

Theo's young brain confused elephant tranquilizers with elephants, and so she waited for the circus to come to town and offer her funny cigarettes.

There had been many moments in the three days of driving that Theo had come close to drinking. Especially when she went into gas station mini-marts and saw all the six-packs of beer in the refrigerators. Staring at them, she knew exactly how each would taste going down her throat. Ever since the first time she stole one of her father's beers in junior high and guzzled it on the side of the house after school, she'd loved the taste.

She wished Olivia was with her and looked at the phone. But she didn't know how to even begin updating Olivia on everything that had happened. She didn't even know about Cary Grant! Then Theo thought about calling Dr. West and filling her in on the dog's progress but it was the middle of the night. Even if she left a message she was afraid it would make her seem unstable. Theo bet Dr. West hadn't spent her after-school hours guzzling beer on the side of the house, and as a result she now lived a meaningful life saving animals. Theo wondered what she would do for work when she got to New York. The thought of cashiering at another party supply store terrified her. She tried to comfort herself by touching one of Cary Grant's ears, but the startled dog woke up and barked.

"Sorry," she said, trying to retract any bad energy.

She gave up on trying to sleep, turned on the light and sat up in bed. The dog glanced over at her, waiting. Theo lit a cigarette and when she exhaled, the dog moved its head to avoid the smoke. Theo picked up the ashtray and moved into the other bed. She was filled with self-loathing. What monster kills their rescue dog with secondhand smoke? She looked at the orange plastic bottle of the dog's painkillers. She needed sleep, and figured the dog would be okay if it missed a few doses. By the time she was asking herself if it still counted as sober if she took the dog's painkillers, she was sobbing—a deep, old wail. Even if Olivia was here with her, she'd still be alone. She needed a hug and Olivia wasn't the hugging type. Still, she dialed Olivia's phone number.

The phone rang and rang. After Theo was all cried out, she got up and walked down the hall to the vending machine. Maybe it was just Coke o'clock, her body demanding sugar to replace the alcohol it was used to. She chugged the cold can of Coke and got back into the bed where Cary Grant had fallen back asleep. The dog was dreaming, and Theo watched her paws flip back and forth as if she was running. She decided to get dressed and go into the casino.

⋮

Theo had grown up in casinos. Her family lived in Las Vegas, and when she was a child she would be left in the video arcade for hours with a roll of quarters. But the quarters were gone in no time, and if the arcade was empty she would wander around pulling on joysticks or pushing start buttons in the hope that suddenly the game would do something. She looked for quarters on the floor, or if other kids were around she watched them beat on the fire button, blowing up asteroids. Every couple of hours a relative would come by to see if she was okay or needed some money to go bowling. She didn't want to go bowling or be in the arcade either, since both places felt like a holding tank. She grew up hating casinos, and it was as if she had some sort of child's x-ray vision: it was so obvious the only point of a casino was to turn everyone into zombies and steal their money.

The other point of casinos was to lose money in order to win points to redeem ugly shit like dinner plates and duffel bags, fleece zip-ups and sets of tacky wine glasses. When Theo had grown up and moved away from home, her aunt would regift many of the things she'd gotten "free" from the casino to her when she visited. The most incomprehensible of all the gifts had been a plastic chute that had double-stick tape on the back. It was supposed to be a toothpaste dispenser; affix it to the bathroom wall and it would hold a tube of toothpaste upside down. Theo couldn't understand why anyone would need it, rich or poor. "Can you use this?" Theo's aunt had asked, handing her the toothpaste dispenser.

"What is it?"

"It holds your toothpaste."

"Okay," Theo said, not wanting to hurt her aunt's feelings.

"You don't know how many people I've tried to give this to. You're the only one who said yes."

There was no going back then.

In the car on the way to the airport Theo's mother said, "I can't believe you want the toothpaste holder."

Theo hadn't known *not* taking the toothpaste holder was a choice, and now she dreaded having it in her possession. She hated clutter and purposefully owned almost nothing. She knew this would be one of those things that remained in its packaging—"Retail Value: $19.99!"—and sat around the apartment collecting dust, a catalyst for a nervous breakdown one day. While waiting for her plane to board, Theo tried to get to the bottom of the mystery. She thought maybe the toothpaste dispenser was meant for rich people; after all, rich people were finicky and needed different things. Like once, in a rich person catalog, Theo had seen a special vacuum for ladies who were very afraid of spiders. The vacuum had a long handle with a snap-on plastic cartridge, and when you sucked up the spider, it stayed in the plastic cartridge. Then you could just throw out the entire cartridge. Theo imagined a landfill filled with plastic cartridges, each holding a single spider. She ended up leaving the toothpaste dispenser in the airport bathroom. Surely, someone could use it.

The first time Theo ever went to a casino on her own was when a drunk Australian dyke on a visit to San Francisco picked her up in a bar and begged her to go on a road trip. She wanted to have an American adventure, so they drove to Reno and got a room. The Australian was young and femme and rich, and she insisted on paying for everything. After some sex and a steak dinner they wandered around the casino, drunk. She gave Theo a hundred-dollar bill at the roulette wheel and Theo plunked down five dollars at a time on her favorite numbers. The Australian was hanging all over her, biting her neck. The first time the ball landed on her number Theo was surprised, but then it just kept happening. That night everything shifted. Maybe casinos were only sad if you didn't have special powers like Theo did: She'd made over four hundred dollars in twenty minutes.

$\vdots$

Theo felt guilty about leaving Cary Grant in the motel room alone while she wandered through the deserted casino. The dog wasn't used to her yet, and she hoped she would just stay asleep and not have some sort of freak-out. Some of her friends' dogs had eaten shower curtains and chewed up entire couches in their absence. She stopped at an empty roulette table and bought twenty dollars' worth of chips. She put five dollars on the number eight and watched the croupier spin the wheel.

Theo had learned about roulette from reading Dostoyevsky's *The Gambler*. Rumor has it that Dostoyevsky wrote that story as a way to get money to pay off a huge gambling debt. Theo believed it—only a true gambler could write the kind of roulette scenes he did, with that perfect mix of blind hope and insanity. The grandmother who can't stop plunking rubles down on zero after just having won on that very number. *Zero. Zero. Zero.* She won't stop saying it. Theo was terrified to turn the page because she knew every winning streak eventually has to come to an end. All of the grandmother's relatives surround her at the table, sickened by her bravado, because if she loses all her money there'll be nothing left to mooch from her.

Theo watched the silver ball jump around the wheel.

"Red seven," the croupier said, setting the marker down next to Theo's chips and throwing her an apologetic look before sweeping them away.

This time she put five dollars on number seven and five dollars on number eight.

"Good luck," the croupier said, spinning the wheel again.

If either of her numbers hit, she would win $175. She watched the ball rattle around while the wheel slowed down, popping into the number eight slot and then out again.

"Black thirteen," the croupier said, dropping his marker and sweeping Theo's chips away again.

She thought about betting thirteen, but decided to push her final five chips to the number eight. If she stopped betting eight now and it hit she'd never forgive herself.

"Good luck," the croupier repeated.

Theo turned her back to the spinning wheel and lit a cigarette. She could hear way off in a corner of the casino the sound of someone vacuuming, then the clicking of the ball in the slots.

"Black thirteen," the croupier called out.

Theo couldn't believe it had come up thirteen two spins

in a row. She gave the croupier a defeated smile and walked away from the table. Since she'd done well the first time she'd ever played roulette, somewhere in her brain she really believed she had a knack for it or that maybe she was somehow able to will the silver ball to nestle into the slots of her favorite numbers. Winning is the worst thing that can happen to a gambler. After that first big win, Theo took the free casino bus from San Francisco to Reno several times a week, telling herself she was doing it to supplement the income from her job as a cashier at the Party Store. There were coupons in the paper that not only made the ride to the casino free, but gave travelers twenty-five dollars in "free" gambling money. She got paid fifty dollars to work a seven-hour shift at the Party Store, so instead of getting a second job, she would try to win a hundred dollars at the casino. The trick was getting out the door with the winnings.

Theo wandered over to a table where a few guys were clapping and yelling. The craps table is always the liveliest table in a casino. She didn't know how to play craps, so she just stood to the side next to a balding white guy wearing a ripped tuxedo T-shirt.

"Cocktails," the cocktail waitress said, stopping next to Theo.

"Coke, please," Theo said.

"Jack and Coke," Tuxedo-tee said.

"You playing?" he asked Theo.

"I don't know how."

"I can show you. I'm trying to quit," he said. "I just got married."

Theo nodded.

"Marriage is a compromise," he told Theo.

She was surprised he was so forthcoming.

"Your best odds in the casino are right here," Tuxedo-tee said, pointing to the craps table. "If you've got two hundred dollars to start with you can practically make a living off this."

"I like easy living," Theo said.

"What's your name?"

"Theo."

"Mark," Tuxedo-tee said. "You got two hundred dollars, Theo?"

Theo nodded.

"You want to learn how to do this?"

"Okay." She counted two hundred dollars in twenties out of her pocket and held the money out to him.

"Put it down on the table," he said, refusing to touch it. "You're going to laugh at how easy this is."

Theo elbowed herself in among the small group of men and exchanged two hundred dollars for three small towers of chips. She could see Mark's eyes getting sweaty as he stood there telling her where to put the bets. He wouldn't touch the chips or the money because then he wasn't technically gambling, just like you're not technically touching the stripper during the lap dance if you keep your hands off her tits. But the gambler in him was alive as he told Theo what numbers to plunk her chips on. One of the rowdy guys threw the dice and everyone groaned. Theo looked at Mark, who signaled for her to put a new stack of chips where she'd just had them.

"Did I win?" Theo asked.

"Not yet," Mark said.

Another rowdy guy threw the dice and Theo watched as they bounced around inside the table.

"Fuck," Mark hissed. "This is the time."

But the result was the same the next five or six times the dice were thrown, until in less than five minutes under Mark's tutelage she'd lost her entire two hundred dollars and still didn't understand how the game worked.

"I've never seen dice so unlucky," Mark said.

It was such a gambler thing to say. Gamblers believe dice are oracles or monks or soothsayers—anything but just white plastic cubes, painted with black dots. Mark followed Theo away from the table and she could see the hunger in his eyes; he didn't want to leave the casino. She wanted to ditch him so she could focus on winning her money back, but she felt weirdly codependent with this stranger. As they walked up and down the rows of slot machines she understood every single step he took, the whole game of trying to walk casually when every cell just wants to hurry up and sit down and shove some goddamned money into a slot machine to feel those bright-colored packets of endorphins hanging like candy bars fall and dissolve in her brain.

There are so many different kinds of video slot machine themes that it shouldn't be hard for anyone to find one that appears to hold their very own destiny. Slot machines with lisping auctioneer bulls, and romantic cats that speak French, and goats that are surgeons. Theo always gravitated toward slot machines with animal themes because one day she wanted to have a small farm with a tiny country house and a duck pond. But instead of saving money for a house where she could have a long, gravel driveway flanked by attack geese, she sat in front of slot machines trying to line up a bunch of geese in tuxedos.

"Please God, please just give me one more goose."

Mark steered them to a Playboy Bunny machine and said, "What about this one?"

Theo had figured she knew the target audience for the Playboy slot machines, and now it was confirmed.

She had forty dollars left in her pocket and pushed it into the bill feeder. She hit the SPIN button wishing with every fiber in her being for a miracle. But, despite Mark saying, "This machine's gonna heat up. Just wait!" she lost her forty dollars in an excruciatingly short amount of time.

"Well, I'm broke," she said, getting up from the slot machine and feeling in her pocket for the room key.

"Oh," Mark said. He seemed surprised, like she was abruptly ending a date and now he was going to have to figure out what to do with his life.

"Goodnight," she said, through with being polite. She headed back to her room.

⋮

Theo had awakened something ugly inside herself, and while she'd managed not to drink she didn't want her new start in New York to be tarnished with her old demons. She felt self-conscious about someone having witnessed her losing money, like an alcoholic who wants to drink at home alone. And she had known, sitting next to Mark, that they were the same, both addicts. The fake nonchalance of just one more spin until all the money's gone. In San Francisco, during some gambling lows she'd sold her clothes, left bills unpaid, written bad checks and gotten money however else she could to be able to stay in the dark casino, pushing a button mindlessly and chain-smoking.

She'd started gambling by playing blackjack. She'd sit at the table and talk to the other players and they rooted each other on to beat the dealer. For as long as she was on a lucky streak and the chips were piling up in her favor everyone was a family of shipwrecked comrades. Her skin became thinner with each hour, until a single drop of alcohol spilt on her wrist could make her feel drunk. She was numb and wired at the same time. She could earnestly think she could fuck and marry everyone sitting at the table around her when she was winning. Even the dealers were on her side. It's not the dealer's money. The dealers wanted her to win so she would throw ridiculous tips at them. The dealers were gambling too, when they weren't working. But when her chips were gone and there wasn't any money left in her pocket to get more, and she'd already done the long walk of shame to the cashier booth or the ATM until there was no money left in those places, either, she would have to wait until midnight, when in the bank's mind it was a new day and her withdrawal limit rolled over. She'd stand behind the other hardcore gamblers, at first shifting her weight from foot to foot, trying to look casual, and then she would stop trying to look casual. She just waited in line with the others with pissed-off or scared expressions.

But there was something about dog track casinos especially that beckoned a certain type of hardcore gambler. No one strolls through the parking lot of a dog track casino; they're rushing to find a place where they can be alone and push a button, or push a pile of chips on a lucky number, or get teary when an ace is turned over in front of them like a healthy baby. Once, when Theo was hurrying to get inside a dog track casino, she passed a flaming car in the parking lot. The fire department hadn't arrived yet. Who knew if anyone had even called the fire department; she didn't. She barely slowed down to double check over her shoulder to make sure her truck was parked far enough away that if the flaming car blew up, hers wouldn't catch fire from the sparks. There were a few people around her, walking past it like zombies too, barely turning their heads to look at the flames. It seemed like all the gamblers were under time constraints or were lying to someone in order to be there. Their kids thought they were out buying groceries or their husbands and wives had been asleep when they had slowly coaxed money from their wallets. And when there was no money left to steal, they set their own cars on fire for the insurance money. They could just light a match, and while it burned, ask the cocktail waitress for a complimentary soda or beer and try to win a little something at the blackjack table.

During the last year in San Francisco, when her drinking really took off, she would take time off from the Party Store and take the bus to the casino every day. She started to recognize other people gambling at the slot machines. At first, she was winning. She was getting free drinks and free money. She felt like she had figured out some great mystery; it was so easy to win a couple hundred dollars. But soon she wasn't able to get home with the money. She thought, if I can win a couple hundred then I can win a couple hundred more, and then she found she would stay until she'd lost all her winnings, or if by some stroke of luck she did make it out the door with the money, then she lost it and more the next day when she returned. Theo wore lucky dice underwear when she went to the casino and a lucky royal flush belt buckle. And in the hours she sat next to other gamblers she'd learn she wasn't the only one wearing special outfits or a piece of jewelry from a dead relative as a charm.

Once Theo sat next to an old woman with short, dyed-black hair who was wearing a leopard leotard and black tights under a giant black parka. Her tiny, wrinkled face was dwarfed behind an extra-large white Styrofoam cup of coffee. She was smoking and she reached over to light Theo's cigarette for her.

"Yesterday, I won," she said, "and when I win, then I wear the same thing again the next day. Because it's lucky," she said, waving her hand over her leotard.

When Theo was losing she didn't want to talk to anyone. But she couldn't resist the tale of the lucky leotard. The woman looked a little deeper into Theo's eyes and told her that she wore a diaper to the casino, a friend told her about it, because that way she could drink as much coffee as she wanted and never get up from the slot machine to pee. Theo wanted to ask if she wore the same diaper, too. After that, two things happened. One, Theo felt much better about her gambling problem because she didn't wear a diaper. And two, she became obsessed with staring at the other gamblers' asses, trying to figure out which ones seemed unnecessarily puffy or crinkly.

About a month before she decided to leave San Francisco Theo had found herself chain-smoking and gambling for sometimes fourteen hours straight, her brain cracking from the barnyard sounds of slot machine animals. She went from roulette to blackjack to the slots. She stopped playing roulette because money went too fast, so she moved on to blackjack for better odds. She'd sit at someone's blackjack table drinking free gin and tonics and playing cards. She'd drink and drink and almost never feel drunk, just heavy and depressed. She fell in love with the kind eyes of the dealers.

Once a dealer looked at her and said, "Are you going to be here my whole shift?"

Theo didn't realize she'd already been playing cards for eight hours. She couldn't leave, she was on such a winning streak that day. When the dealer's shift was over Theo stayed, and with the new dealer she managed to lose everything.

⋮

On the way back to her room Theo scanned the carpet for money, a quarter even. She found she was religious in casinos: If God loved her he'd let her find a quarter on the carpet, and she would use that quarter to try just one more time, drop it into a slot machine and hit the jackpot. But, deep down she knew no one hit the jackpot on a quarter they found on the rug. Ever.

When she opened the door to the motel room, Cary Grant looked up from where she was sleeping in a tight circle at the end of the bed. Theo was relieved that the dog hadn't had some kind of freak-out in her absence.

"Hi," she said, sitting down next to her.

The dog watched her. Theo felt exhausted and lay down with the light on, fully dressed, her feet hanging off the edge of the bed. A flare of anger surged through her at her stupidity for losing two hundred and forty dollars. She got up and fished a bright yellow Café Bustelo can out of her bag. She took the lid off and removed the wad of perfectly organized bills, counting the money as Cary Grant watched. She had seven hundred and ten dollars. She counted out two hundred and forty dollars and put it in her pocket. All she would have to do is go back to the roulette wheel and put the entire sum on black or red. She had a fifty-fifty chance of winning her losses back with a single spin. Very gently, she laid her hand on the dog's side.

"I'll be right back," she told Cary Grant.

When she rose the dog followed her to the door and

stood beside her, tail wagging. Theo glanced at the night-stand clock. It was 4 AM.

"Time for bed?" Theo asked.

And she turned off the light and got back in bed with Cary Grant.

The next morning Theo forced herself to get on the road and not entertain the idea of staying one more day at the casino motel. She drove straight to New York, stopping only when absolutely necessary to nap in a rest area. Cary Grant had officially bonded to her and started to lean against her or put her paw on Theo's leg while she was driving. Theo attributed the progress to the small fortune she'd spent on hot dogs.

New York looked like she'd imagined it: gridlock, clusters of tall, brick apartment buildings and swatches of colorful bubbled graffiti on passing delivery trucks. She realized, sitting in traffic on the Tappan Zee Bridge, that she'd reached her destination and now she didn't know where to go. This was the moment Olivia had been hounding her about. What would she do when she got to New York? Where would she live? She'd thought Olivia was being a downer or was jealous or hurt by her leaving. Theo had spent so many hours imagining her New York apartment that it had never occurred to her she still needed to find one.

She imagined the same modest apartment that characters in movies got when they moved to New York to start a new life: a few small rooms with gleaming hardwood floors and a claw-foot tub. A fire escape off the kitchen where she could start a small collection of red geraniums. A humble view of the Brooklyn Bridge. The first exit after the Tappan Zee Bridge she'd buy a Coke, and walk Cary Grant, and find a pay phone to call the one person she knew in New York, an Italian dyke with a dark mop of hair named Sammy.

The hairball of interlocking parkways and overpasses confused her, and Theo drove for twenty minutes, somehow looping back to where she started. The next time she went a different way, until the clusters of tall apartment buildings disappeared and she found herself driving along lush greenery where tiny bridges fed people off the expressway and into towns that looked stuck in the 1950s. The third time she looped another wrong way and found herself about to pay the toll again at the Tappan Zee Bridge.

She put her hazards on in the emergency lane and got out and lit a cigarette. If she got a ticket for stopping traffic at least maybe the cop could tell her what direction she needed to go. She lifted Cary Grant out and walked along the gravel shoulder to let her pee. The dog relieved herself then dipped her head to stretch.

"We're lost," she said, and Cary Grant wagged.

"Let's find a place to live," she said, loading the dog back in the truck.

The toll booth employee gave Theo directions to get out of the bad loop, and she followed the signs pointing toward the Bronx. Then she pulled over at the first convenience store she saw.

"Progress," she said to Cary Grant, who now became excited each time the truck stopped.

The dog wagged when Theo opened the glove compartment to get out her address book. That's where she'd stored the hot dogs on the drive across country, but there were no hot dogs left. She opened her phone book and found Sammy's number under "S" with the words "Sammy Jail."

Theo and Sammy had met at a rally protesting the acquittal of the cops who beat Rodney King. Sammy was visiting San Francisco from New York and hadn't planned to go to the protest, had just been smoking pot in the park when she got swept up with the other protesters and arrested. During thirty hours of wrongful incarceration they'd become friends. When they were released Sammy had given Theo her number and said, "If you're ever in New York. . . ."

Theo hadn't known if Sammy was trying to flirt with her, but now Theo was in New York with nowhere to live and a pit bull that had been thrown off a roof. She dialed Sammy's number, and someone answered on the second ring.

"Sammy?" Theo asked, trying to remember her voice.

"Who's this?" a woman with a thick New York accent said.

"Theo."

Theo heard children screaming at each other in the background.

"We met in jail when she was visiting San Francisco."

As soon as the words came out of Theo's mouth she regretted saying them.

"Oh yeah," the woman said cheerily, "She told me about that. She's working on a fishing boat right now."

"Oh."

Theo was at a loss.

"Do you want to leave your number?"

"I don't have one yet. If you talk to her can you tell her I moved to New York?"

"Sure. Make sure to stay outta jail," the woman said, cackling, before she hung up the phone.

Theo stared at the pay phone trying to come up with a plan to find a job and a place to live, now that the one person she knew was off working on a fishing boat. She left Cary Grant in the truck and went into the Kwik Stop to buy a Coke and cigarettes and hot dogs. Theo brought everything to the register and stared at the acne on the skinny cashier's chin.

"Hi," he said.

"Hi," Theo replied.

She added a local newspaper to her pile of things.

"Can you tell me the name of this town?" she asked.

He looked surprised by her question.

"Yonkers."

"I'm still in New York, right?"

"That depends on who you ask."

three

Theo needed to get a job. She drove through Yonkers stopping at every business with a HELP WANTED sign while Cary Grant watched out the window, anticipating each return. When she ran out of the will to walk into strange, sad Yonkers businesses and ask about a job, Theo took the dog to a park and perused the classified ads for apartments; most were too expensive and didn't allow dogs.

The pay phone in the Kwik Stop parking lot became her office. She called a phone number for a $300 room in Yonkers, and when the answering machine picked up she realized she didn't have a call-back number, so she left the pay phone number and said she'd be available after 5 PM.

Theo looked for jobs some more, and then returned at 5 PM. Placing Cary Grant's bowls on the ground next to her truck, she waited for the phone to ring. The day already felt like a week. Having nowhere to live, or just to be, made the hours stretch on forever. Theo wasted two hours waiting for the pay phone to ring and then drove around to find a park to sleep for the night. She reclined her seat and placed her hand on Cary Grant's rib cage, feeling it lift slightly each time the dog inhaled. She used it as a kind of meditation and drifted into a tense slumber as her psyche waited for cops to show up and tell her to move along, or for a psycopath to crawl out of the bushes and kill her.

When sleeping in her truck on the cross-country drive she hadn't thought of herself as homeless, just economical. Now that she was no longer in transit, one day of washing her face and brushing her teeth at the train station had filled her with despair.

Over the next couple days, when not applying for jobs or housing or getting lost in the hairball of Westchester County highways, Theo casually wandered supermarket aisles, stuffing thirty-cent rolls in her mouth and chewing them as quickly as possible, afraid to spend any cash in case she needed it for a room deposit. The only groceries she bought were a can opener and four cans of baked beans, twenty-five cents each. She was trying to combat a constant headache, the result of hunger, or smoking too much, or a combination of the two.

Theo filled out job applications, sometimes ten a day, listing the pay phone as her home number with specific instructions to call only after 5 PM. After a particularly demoralizing rejection for a cashier position at a Friendly's diner, she splurged and bought a grape soda and two hot dogs from a man who had a cart near the park. Cary Grant inhaled her hot dog and then gave Theo's wrist a tiny lick to say *thank you*. Rejuvenated, she went back to her plan to Make It in New York.

That evening when she returned to the pay phone she saw a HELP WANTED sign in the window of the convenience store. She practically ran inside, smiling at the acne-faced cashier who now knew her pretty well from coming in and out all day for coffee and cigarettes and classified ads.

"You're hiring?"

He nodded. "My cousin just went back to school and quit with no notice, and no one else in my family wants to work here."

"Oh."

"It's my uncle's store. Have you ever cashiered before?" he asked shyly.

"Yes. I've cashiered a lot."

"I'm Randy," he said, extending his bony hand, but Theo already knew the thin boy's name from his nametag. *Randy, Manager.*

"I just moved here from San Francisco."

Randy's eyes lit up.

"I've always wanted to go to California," which Theo interpreted as, *I'm young and gay and stuck in Yonkers, help!*

He looked barely eighteen.

Theo started the application, leaving phone number and address blank.

"Do you think you could you start tomorrow morning," Randy asked, "because I have a dentist appointment."

"Really?" Theo said, relief flooding her body.

"Is that okay? Or do you have something to do?"

"That's perfect."

"It's minimum wage but you can have as many hot dogs and sodas as you want. And coffee."

"That sounds great."

"We have to wear this uniform," Randy said, sadly pulling at his turquoise smock.

"That's okay."

Randy looked at Theo and said, "Do you want the boy smock or the girl smock? The boy one is better," he added quickly.

"The boy one then," Theo said, relieved.

She watched him dart into a supply closet and emerge with two turquoise smocks enclosed in plastic wrap.

"So what time should I come in tomorrow?"

"Six."

"Thanks, Randy."

"I have a feeling you're going to be great."

Cary Grant's ears perked up as she saw Theo approach. Theo opened the truck door and gave the dog a quick hug, whispering in her ear, "I got us a job that includes all the hot dogs we can eat!"

The dog thumped her tail hard into the seat as Theo kissed her ears. She was still cooing in the dog's face when she heard the pay phone.

"Hello?"

"Is this Theo?" a gruff female voice asked.

"Yes."

"This is Doralina. You called about the room."

"Which one is this?"

"Three hundred dollars. Yonkers."

"Oh yeah," Theo said. "Is it possible to take a look at it?"

"You have a dog, right?"

"Yes."

"Does it pee in the house?"

"No," Theo paused. "It's a special dog. She was thrown off a roof."

"A roof?"

She started telling Doralina the dog's story in an attempt to make her sympathetic, but then realized she sounded crazy. Only unstable people lived where dogs were thrown off roofs. Theo had to convince her. It was already September. What would happen when winter came and it was too cold for them to sleep in the truck?

"Is the room available now?" Theo asked.

"Yeah, it's just sitting empty."

"Could I come look at it?" Theo tried to not sound desperate.

"You got a job, right?"

"Totally," Theo said.

"Where at?"

Theo read the sign aloud: "The Kwik Stop," she said. "Right before you get on the expressway."

"Oh. I've probably seen you. I live just down the street. You want to come over now?"

Theo drove to the address Doralina gave her and left Cary Grant in the truck. She rang the doorbell twice, and eventually a dykey white woman wearing giant gray sweatpants opened the door. She looked Theo up and down, obviously surprised to find queerness on her own front step.

Yonkers was a fucking time warp. Every place Theo had applied for a job she'd felt *GAY*, and had to ignore the gawker stares. When the eventual sirma'amsir documentary was made, Yonkers would be the new habitat where Theo finds herself uncamouflaged, waiting to be plucked and eaten by a hate-criming, carnivorous bird.

When she left San Francisco Theo had thought she didn't care if she ever saw a gay pride flag again. Sometimes she'd even wanted to scream, "Put some goddamned pants on!" at the men who walked down the sidewalk in assless chaps. But the gay people in Yonkers seemed to lack not just gay pride, but gay ambition. A week removed from the gay mecca, and Theo was already fantasizing about founding a gay support group for pimple-faced Randy and dykey Doralina.

Doralina led Theo up two flights of stairs to a small attic room with a slanted roof that was just big enough to accommodate her futon. The floor was covered in bright red carpet the color of Ronald McDonald's hair. A tiny airplane-size window hung like a painting where the slanted ceiling met the wall.

"I love it," Theo said after standing in the room for ten seconds.

Doralina seemed surprised.

"Most people think it's too small."

"I don't have that much stuff," Theo said. "Do you want to meet my dog?"

"Okay."

Theo wondered if Doralina was on heavy drugs. There was something very underwater about her.

They walked back downstairs, and Theo rolled down the window so Doralina could see Cary Grant.

"It's a pit bull?" Doralina said.

"I think so."

"They bite kids?"

Cary Grant watched Doralina.

"She's never bitten a child," Theo said, unsure if that was true.

"Does she bark?" Doralina asked.

In the week that Theo had had the dog the only noise she'd ever heard her make was the yelp when she was thrown onto the Taco Lady's tarp.

"No, she's a good dog."

Doralina reached through the window to pet Cary Grant but the dog ducked away from her hand.

"She's shy," Theo offered.

"Just lock her up when my son comes over. I don't need no hospital bills."

Theo was surprised by the news of Dykey Doralina's

kid, and for a second she wondered if she was wrong about her being gay.

"When are you looking to move in?" Doralina asked.

Theo didn't want to let on that she was homeless. She also didn't want to spend another night sleeping in her truck.

"I could move in now," Theo said, "as long as I'm here."

"It's six hundred dollars for rent and deposit," Doralina said in a tough voice, almost like a challenge.

Theo reached under the driver's seat for her coffee can. She counted six hundred dollars in twenty-dollar bills. The can was almost empty, and a wave of panic went through her. She'd count exactly how much was left later when she was alone. She'd gotten a job and a place to live, and while many would interpret a cashier position at a convenience store and a tiny room in a Yonkers apartment as fucking dismal, Theo knew in her bones that life was looking up.

Doralina helped Theo drag the futon and boxes up to her room. Within an hour her belongings were put away and she'd put sheets on her bed. Cary Grant lay on the bright red carpet in a tight circle watching Theo's every move. Theo couldn't wait to take a shower. She unpacked her duffel bag looking for clean underwear and saw the wig. It made her miss Olivia deeply. She hung it on the doorknob and went to the bathroom to fill Cary Grant's water dish. The dog thumped her tail into the wall excitedly when she returned with the blue bowl. She lapped at the water shyly, casting her nervous eyes at Theo.

Theo imagined her new room as Vincent Van Gogh's famous painting of his Arles bedroom; instead of a four-poster bed, she had a navy blue futon mattress, and instead of a wood-plank floor, Ronald McDonald–red carpet. Instead of a tiny mirror with thin, vertical, brushstrokes of color, Theo had a mirror-size window right below the attic eaves. If Van Gogh came back from the dead to paint Theo's new bedroom she bet he'd mute the carpet and use the light blue dog dishes as the focal point—all the energy swirling out of those two faded periwinkle bowls.

When Cary Grant fell asleep on the futon, Theo carefully removed the stitches on her side with a nail clipper. She woke feeling Theo pull the first stitch, but tolerated the medical assistance. Theo tiptoed to the bathroom so she wouldn't disturb the dog, and felt the luxury of grooming herself outside a train station restroom. She returned to her bedroom, set her tiny alarm clock for 5 AM and climbed into bed. When she was settled, the dog got up and repositioned herself, settling with her head against Theo's leg.

"You're my best friend," Theo said to her.

Tomorrow while she was at work Cary Grant would have her own room to limp around in. She loved the dog's nervous brown eyes and planned to celebrate their new life together after work. She'd take some of those free hot dogs and go to the park where Cary Grant could walk slowly through the grass with her cast, sniffing at the wildflowers, and she could watch the sun set.

⋮

Theo arrived at the Kwik Stop at 6 AM. The turquoise smock felt heavy on her chest, like an x-ray vest. Randy told her to make herself a cup of coffee and then trained her on the cash register, selling lottery tickets, and lining up the new hot dogs on the rolling grill. She made a fresh pot of coffee in each flavor, and then after three hours Randy left her to get his cavity filled.

The store was busy, and Theo rang up rush-hour customers with their coffees and cigarettes and breakfast bur-
ritos and beef jerky. She couldn't believe how much beef
jerky she sold—as if all of Yonkers was fueled by it. When it
slowed down she browsed the classified ads and called about
a few jobs. Now that she had a job, maybe she could find another one that paid more than minimum wage. Or maybe she
could have two jobs and afford her own apartment. She dialed
the number for an ad that read DATA ENTRY NO EXPERIENCE
NECESSARY and scheduled an interview for later that day.

When Randy returned with his numb mouth, he seemed
astounded that Theo had actually done the things he'd asked.

He kept saying, "You remembered to put the hot dogs
out? You remembered to make the coffee?"

"Yes," Theo said, feeling sad that some people couldn't
remember that much.

When her shift was over he packed her a bag with four
hot dogs and a 64-ounce Coke.

"Same time tomorrow?" he said smiling.

Theo was the friend he'd been waiting forever to meet.

"Same time," she confirmed.

Theo was so excited to see Cary Grant she practically
bounded up the stairs when she got home. She was nervous
to find out if the dog had had an accident or eaten a pillow,
but the room was undisturbed and she found the dog sleeping in her trademark tiny circle.

"Let's go!" Theo said, changing out of her turquoise
smock and putting the dog on a leash.

They went to the park and each ate two hot dogs. Theo
sat on the bench drinking the entirety of her 64-ounce soda
while Cary Grant sniffed around in the grass. Could a dog
really moor a person? Ever since she'd taken Cary Grant on

she'd felt she had an ally. The dog's health was in Theo's hands, and she loved how each day she noticed the small progress she made earning her trust.

The data entry interview was in a strip of factories and business offices. When Theo finally found the right building she parked, leaving Cary Grant in the car. She began to feel depressed just walking toward the building. There was nothing like a cluster of beige business offices to make a person's soul die. Inside, a tall man with thick dark hair and a T-shirt with a cartoon frog that said *boricua* introduced himself to her as Joseph. He led Theo into his office and moved a bunch of catalogs off a chair so she could sit down.

"We sell semiconductors," he barked.

Theo nodded in a meaningful way pretending to know what that meant.

"So let's cut the shit and get to the questions. How fast can you type?"

"Pretty fast," Theo lied.

"You show up to work on time?"

"Always."

"Can you start tomorrow?"

Theo nodded again.

"It's Monday through Friday nine to five. Eight dollars an hour. Don't even think about asking for more because I won't give it to you. Work here for a while and then we'll talk about a raise."

She was only getting $6.50 working at the Kwik Stop.

"You're not pregnant are you?" Joseph asked.

"What?"

"Last girl quit because she was pregnant. And we'd just finally gotten her trained."

"I'm not pregnant."

"Are you sure?" Joseph asked. Then he laughed. "Just kidding. Don't sue me for saying that. And even if you tried I could afford a better lawyer. Okay, you're hired."

He led Theo through the office, introducing her to a few people.

"This will be your office," he said, flipping on a light switch.

It was a windowless room that held only a metal desk and a large gray computer monitor where a green cursor flashed despondently.

"That's my office in there," Joseph said, pointing through a square hole in the wall.

He explained that he'd drop faxes filled with numerical codes for semiconductors and their prices through the hole. Theo's job would be to pick them up off the carpet and enter them into the giant computer.

"A monkey could do this job," Joseph said. "You'll love it."

Next to the stack of faxes on the desk was a large pink ashtray shaped like a pair of lungs. She was thrilled at the thought of smoking at work. Everyone at the office was smoking.

Joseph pointed at the pile of messy faxes, thick as a phone book.

"That's like half a day's faxes. You gotta type fast."

"Okay," Theo said. "Can I bring my dog with me to work?"

"I don't give a fuck, as long as you can type."

"Thank you," Theo said, shaking Joseph's hand and walking out of the office feeling terrified of her new boss.

"Cary Grant, I got another job," she told the dog, who was licking the bloodstains on Theo's old T-shirt.

Theo drove by the Kwik Stop on the way home and told Randy she'd found another job. She wondered if a lot of people only worked there one day.

"But you were so good with the hot dogs," he whined.

"I'm so sorry. This other job pays more."

Randy pulled the HELP WANTED sign out from under the register and walked over to the window to put it up again.

"Will you come visit me sometimes and tell me stories about California?" he asked.

"Sure."

She realized she wanted to save Randy, but dreaded being his only friend.

"Here," he said giving her two ice-cream sandwiches. "It's an early Christmas bonus."

"I'll see you soon," Theo said.

She took the chocolate off one ice-cream sandwich and gave Cary Grant the vanilla middle while she ate the other.

"Tomorrow, it's bring your dog-daughter to work day," she said to the dog, touching the thick scar on its head with her fingertips.

⋮

Theo's optimism dissolved after a few weeks of living her new life in Yonkers. She spent her work days listening to Joseph call everyone and everything, "You. Fucking. Faggot." The faggot could be his brother, a pen, or the price a vendor quoted him. Theo filled a pad with tiny hash marks every time she heard him say, "You. Fucking. Faggot." Besides being able to chain-smoke, the only good things about her job were the ceramic lung ashtray, Cary Grant sleeping all day on a blanket next to her desk, and a sales rep who brought a pink box of donuts with him when he visited once a week. On those glorious days Theo would sneak into the break room, hunch over the pink box, and cram as many donuts as possible into her mouth.

Everyone at work was insane. There was Mimi, the book-keeper, who only wore nylon sweat suits. When she walked through the office Theo heard the swooshing sound of two plastic bags rubbing together. On Fridays Mimi's husband picked her up wearing the men's version of her sweat suit.

Theo wanted to say to Mimi, "I see you're in a same-sweat-suit relationship. Please let me know if you ever need to talk about it."

Both sweat suits had perfect creases down the front of each leg, and Theo wondered if they'd been ironed. She had never understood "twinning" in relationships, and before she met Mimi she'd thought only lesbians dressed alike after years of being together. When Theo was twenty she'd gone to the March on Washington for Gay Rights, and the thing that left the biggest impression on her was seeing two retired gym teachers, both wearing perfect, right-out-of-the-box, matching Marlboro black-and-red track suits. Theo knew the Marlboro catalog they'd gotten them from; she'd looked through it herself. Each empty pack of cigarettes counted for five miles. A person could save the Marlboro miles and buy things like radios or track suits or pool tables—all emblazoned with the Marlboro logo. Everyone wanted the pool table, but the millions of "miles" it took pretty much insured early emphysemic death.

Mimi split her time between paying the company's bills late and writing fraudulent complaint letters to a company that sold the squeaky toys she bought for her white Yorkie with the omnipresent eye boogers. She confided in Theo that every few years she wrote the company demanding compensation for her dog almost choking to death on one of their faulty toys. Like clockwork, a few weeks later she'd receive an enormous box of complimentary dog toys.

Mimi was adamant that none of the company's bills should get paid before the due date. She threw out all the pre-printed envelopes that came enclosed with each bill and instead placed the check in a plain envelope with a handwritten address. When Theo asked her why she did this, Mimi explained that the pre-printed barcodes allowed the post office to deliver the payments speedily, but she didn't want anyone to get their money until the last possible second.

Much of the time at work Theo pretended to be a political prisoner penning groundbreaking poems such as "How Data Entry Can Make You an Alcoholic." So far, she'd managed to not drink or gamble since she'd been in New York, but a craving for alcohol had crawled back, and each time she went into the Kwik Stop to buy cigarettes and say hi to Randy, she found herself hovering longer and longer in front of the sliding glass doors where the six-packs of beer lived.

Her fear of consequences kept her from buying the beer. There had been many consequences over the years: arrests, lost girlfriends, a mental hospital stay, but the thing that scared Theo more than anything was a suicidal streak that popped up unexpectedly when she was drunk. It could sneak out of nowhere. She'd be at parties laughing with friends when the next thing she knew she found herself crawling onto roofs or rifling through strangers' medicine cabinets. It was unfortunate to do these things at sixteen, but at nearly thirty—forget it.

Theo was starting to realize why her room cost only three hundred dollars. Doralina had converted a pantry off the kitchen into a tiny bedroom and hung a curtain for a door, and she'd stay in her cave smoking menthol cigarettes and watching sports all day on TV. Theo quickly figured out that not only did Doralina pay no rent by subletting the rooms, she'd increased the number of them so she was making a profit. When Theo went into the kitchen to make one of her bowls of oatmeal she'd hear Doralina cheering for or against some team through the curtain. She tried to avoid Doralina, because she always wanted a ride somewhere or for Theo to lend her money.

Doralina's best friend, Megan, lived across the hall from Theo, where she kept what seemed like ten million rabbits in cages. In letters to Olivia, Theo referred to Megan as "the rabbit hoarder." The rabbit hoarder worked at a bank and dated a bunch of noncommittal men who all had the same shellacked hair. One rainy day Megan's car broke down and she devised a plan to go to a Saturn Dealership with Doralina and purposely slip in the parking lot, hoping to get a free car. When she had no other choice, Theo made small talk with Megan and Doralina, but mostly she hid in her room with Cary Grant.

Two paydays after she started her data entry job she could finally afford a vet visit to get Cary Grant's cast removed. The dog's skinny leg look naked without its pink cast, and Theo bought a package of hamburger meat to celebrate its removal. Theo had lost weight since she'd moved to New York, the result of a combination of not drinking alcohol and being broke. Between doing data entry five days a week and sometimes helping Randy on the weekends at the Kwik Stop, she couldn't understand how she was still having a hard time making ends meet. It was just expensive to be alive; at least that's what Theo had told her customers when she worked at the Party Store and they were surprised by how much things cost.

Each day after work, while the dog wandered around the dog park, Theo read a few pages of *Lust for Life: The Biography of Vincent Van Gogh.* It inspired her to buy a small sketchbook and a box of charcoals. Sometimes she'd sit on the bench and try to capture the variety of poses the dogs made while playing. She loved how filthy the charcoal made her hands and the sound of it moving across the paper, how the smooth page ate up the marks. Eventually the park would fill up with people and someone would make small talk with Theo, especially a carpenter named Danny. He was a stocky white guy with blond hair and a steel-gray pit bull named Baby. A few weeks after seeing each other every day at the park he asked Theo out to dinner. She was shocked. She didn't know if he had a dyke fetish or if the dating pool in Yonkers was slim pickings. Theo coveted his expensive work boots, endured boring dinner conversation, and watched him get drunk on margaritas while she devoured baskets of chips and salsa at the local travesty of a Mexican restaurant. Even Theo, who was no food connoisseur, knew there was no such thing as a good burrito in Yonkers. When she went on these "dates" with Danny she ate her burrito quickly, letting it slide down her throat the way a snake eats a rat.

four

Around Thanksgiving, when Theo had lived in Yonkers almost three months, she remembered she'd never called Sammy back. Surely she was done working on a fishing boat by now. Theo dialed her number.

"Sammy?" Theo said.

"Yes?"

"It's Theo, from jail."

"Oh my God! My aunt told me you called," Sammy said excitedly, "but you didn't leave a number. Is it true you're in New York?"

"Sort of. I'm in Yonkers," Theo joked.

"Yonkers?"

"It's a long story."

"When are you coming to Brooklyn next?"

In fact, Theo had never left Yonkers since she'd arrived, simply accepting her self-imposed prison.

"My aunt is going to be gone this weekend. Do you want to come down and stay with me?"

"You live with your aunt?"

"For now."

"I could come down after work Friday. Is it okay if I bring my dog?"

"Sure," Sammy said.

When Friday came, she packed a small duffel bag and loaded Cary Grant into the truck, following Sammy's directions carefully. The closer she got to Brooklyn the more alive Theo felt. How was it she'd moved to New York three months ago and never ventured beyond Yonkers? She'd been like a person lost in a snowstorm who tries to survive by burning car tires. When there are no more tires they hike out for help, but they're found shirtless in the snow, dead from hypothermia. The whole time, had they just turned left instead of right, they would've found the ranger station. Theo saw the outline of the Brooklyn Bridge and thought, *My help was here all along*. She felt suddenly invigorated.

Sammy's aunt lived between Bensonhurst and Coney Island on the fourteenth floor in one of a cluster of low-income brick apartment towers. Theo found the right building and led Cary Grant into an elevator that smelled like burning plastic. When the elevator moved, the dog leaned its nervous body against Theo's leg.

"It's okay," she said.

Theo located Sammy's apartment number and rang the doorbell, suddenly nervous.

"Hey girl," Sammy said opening the door.

"Hi, girl," Theo answered, even though they both looked like men.

Sammy had a fast metabolism that left her with a skeletal frame. Theo hugged her slight body.

"Who's this?" Sammy said, leaning down to pet the dog.

"Cary Grant."

"No way!"

"See her little part?" Theo pointed to the scar.

"*North by Northwest* is one of my favorite movies."

"I've never seen it," Theo said.

"That's insane. I own it. We can watch it today."

Cary Grant investigated the apartment while Sammy returned to her bowl of Cocoa Puffs.

"Want a bowl?" Sammy asked holding up her cereal.

"No, I'm good."

Theo looked at the family portraits on the living room wall. One showed a young Sammy sitting at the same kitchen table eating cereal.

"Look, you're eating cereal here too," Theo said.

Sammy laughed. "I haven't done much with my life."

"Did you grow up in this apartment?"

"Pretty much. My aunt and I have shared it since my mom died. But next month I have to find a place because her fiancé is moving in with his kids."

"Where will you go?"

"Somewhere in Brooklyn. That's why I worked on the fishing boat, because I knew I would need a deposit. You should move to Brooklyn."

"That would be so amazing."

"Whatever happens, you can't stay in Yonkers. There aren't even gay people there."

Theo didn't want to end up like Randy or Doralina. She remembered how happy she'd been when she saw the Brooklyn Bridge.

"Have you had any good Brooklyn pizza yet?" Sammy asked.

"This is the first time I've even been to Brooklyn."

"What?! There's this great place: L&B Pizzeria—we

could get some squares, they have a spumoni garden. We could watch *North by Northwest.*"

Sammy walked over to Cary Grant curled up on the couch.

"It's your biggest film, right?" she said to the dog.

Sammy was traditionally good-looking in that Italian kind of way. She had thick dark hair and brown eyes with a Mediterranean complexion. She was rail thin, all ribs and clavicles. If she cleaned up she could play the role of a dashing butch in the one Hollywood film per decade that featured lesbians.

Theo sat down on the couch. She felt happy, looking out the windows that led to Sammy's balcony, with a view of Brooklyn. Sammy petted the dog slowly and then sat up and started rolling a joint.

"Do you smoke?" she asked Theo.

"Only cigarettes," Theo said, afraid to tell Sammy she was sober.

"That's cool," Sammy said, lighting the joint.

Theo watched Sammy as she lay back on the couch with her joint. She envied Sammy's coal-dark eyes and felt confused about whether she wanted to be her or have sex with her. They sat on the couch for a while petting the dog, and when Sammy was properly stoned they headed out for pizza. Theo drove, Cary Grant sat squished in the middle and Sammy pointed out a variety of personal Brooklyn landmarks, including where she'd gone to high school, a deli she worked at where someone was killed in a robbery, and her first boyfriend's house.

Theo loved Brooklyn. She loved the cars driving by with shiny rims and pumping music, she loved the Coney Island silhouettes of roller coasters against the night sky, and when they arrived at L&B Pizzeria and Spumoni Gardens she loved the man in the marinara-soaked apron who expertly slid two corner squares of pizza out of the pan with a spatula and tipped them onto their plates.

Sammy insisted on paying, pulling a wad of "fishing boat money" out of her pocket. They found a free table on the patio where Cary Grant wouldn't be tormented by foot traffic, and Theo raised a grape soda in a toast.

"To Brooklyn," she said.

"And fishing boat money," Sammy said, raising her can of beer.

The pizza was delicious, thick and cheesy, and Theo inhaled her piece, saving a bit of crust for Cary Grant.

"The problem with Yonkers—" Theo started.

"Is everything?" Sammy asked.

They laughed.

"Sort of. It has no life force—everyone seems depressed."

Theo told Sammy about Doralina, and everyone at her awful data entry job, and sweet Randy from the Kwik Stop. Sammy laughed in horror. For the first time since she moved to New York Theo felt like she was talking to a real person instead of trying to hide her freakishness. Sammy told Theo how she'd been so seasick working on the fishing boat at first, how people made illegal hooch and everyone had affairs with each other. She'd never do it again, she said; the work was too grueling even if at the end she had gotten a giant Ed McMahon Sweepstakes–size check.

"I thought the easy money would be a little easier if you know what I mean."

Afterwards, they got ice cream. Theo ordered pistachio and Sammy got two vanilla cones, one for her and one for Cary Grant. Sammy got back in line for the third time and ordered a bag of garlic knots and zeppoles to take home.

"Movie snacks," she said to Theo, holding up the bag.

"I love zeppoles."

When they got back to Sammy's apartment, Cary Grant, who seemed to trust Sammy instinctively, curled up between them to watch *North by Northwest*.

"We're honored to be sitting next to you," Sammy said as the opening credits came up. And then each time the real Cary Grant came on screen she smoothed the top of the dog's head gently and said, "Oh, you look so dapper, Cary."

After the movie, Sammy gave Theo a pillow and blanket for the couch and then went off to sleep herself.

The next day they lazed about eating Cocoa Puffs, and in the late morning they drove to Prospect Park. The street lamps were decorated with Christmas garland. It was sunny but chilly as they walked over the stiff grass, Cary Grant sniffing the trees. Sammy went into a deli at the edge of the park and got two roast beef and provolone sandwiches, potato salad, and more grape soda while Theo waited outside with the dog. They ate in the truck with the heat on, Cary Grant strategically in front of the heater, warming her fur.

Being in Brooklyn and having a friend was making Theo even more depressed about Yonkers.

"I never want to go back," she told Sammy.

"You want me to ask my aunt if you can crash with us for a little while?" Sammy asked. "The only thing is you'd have to sleep on the floor. Because we just have the couch and her bedroom."

"But I don't have a job here," Theo said. "Or any money."

"We should find an apartment together. If we shared a one-bedroom we could afford it. You could get out of Yonkers. I could help you take care of Cary Grant."

"Really?" Theo asked. "Will a one-bedroom be big enough?"

"We could get a pull-out couch for the living room and trade off the bedroom every few months. When I'm not at massage school I'll probably be at work anyway."

The prospect of having someone to help her pay the rent and take care of the dog was exciting.

"Let's get some beer and the classifieds and look for some apartments right now," Sammy said.

"Okay."

She didn't want to tell Sammy she was trying to be sober, because the idea of a beer sounded amazing. Theo had many sobriety dates: August 1st, March 18th, September 3rd, September 18th, New Year's Day (Theo's birthday January 1st), every old girlfriend's birthday, her mother's birthday, and after she fell in love with Vincent Van Gogh, March 30th, his birthday. The great thing about quitting drinking so many times, she told herself, was it gave her a kind of expertise to know how to stop again if she relapsed. Her alcoholism was like a person who finds themselves running down a too-steep hill; inevitably their body moves faster than their legs and they plummet face-first into the gravel. No, she wasn't going to tell Sammy she was sober, just in case she decided to drink.

Theo drove them through Brooklyn back to Sammy's, riding a manic high at the prospect of drinking again. Her body turned jumpy the way it did when she flirted with unavailable girls or considered stealing; she was tiptoeing on the edge of danger. The mania made all of Brooklyn brighter—the butcher shops and corner stores and clusters of old men sitting on park benches reading the *New York Post*.

Back at Sammy's apartment, Sammy rolled a joint.

"Oh, I forgot to get the beer," Sammy said taking a hit off her joint.

"It's no big deal," Theo said, trying to seem nonchalant.

Theo read the apartment ads out loud to Sammy one at a time, circling every one that was less than $800. Then Sammy and Theo alternated calling. Each time someone answered, the apartment had already been rented.

"But the paper only came out today. I don't understand—how is everything already rented?" Theo said.

"We'll find a place," Sammy reassured her. "It's only the first day."

In the late afternoon they went to Coney Island, and even though the boardwalk was closed for the winter they managed to buy some Nathan's cheese fries. They walked the perimeter of the locked-up rides, looking at the tall weeds growing through the concrete at the foot of the Cyclone Rollercoaster.

"Have you ever been on that?" Theo asked Sammy.

Sammy nodded.

"We can come here in the summer when it's open. You feel like you're going to die. It's so fun."

"Has anyone ever died on it?"

"Yeah. A couple."

Sammy pointed to the roller coaster's wooden planks. "Don't they look like they could snap in half any minute?"

On the drive home, Sammy pointed out more Brooklyn landmarks as night fell. Finally, when it was time for Theo to go home, her stomach filled with dread. Sammy promised to continue looking for apartments on their behalf and gave Cary Grant a big hug good-bye. The dog looked out the window at Sammy as they pulled away. As Theo drove up the FDR she watched the Brooklyn Bridge get smaller in her rearview mirror. She vowed to find a job in Brooklyn as soon as possible so she could leave that shit hole, Yonkers.

five

Everything about life in Yonkers felt like a punishment now. She hated Doralina, who'd taken to knocking on her bedroom door late at night and sitting dramatically on the futon.

"This is really hard for me, because I have a lot of shame," Doralina would start, "but can I borrow twenty dollars until my check comes?"

Theo didn't believe it was hard for Doralina to ask for money, since she seemed to do it several times a week. She hadn't had any extra money since she'd moved to New York, and if she came into some she sure as shit wasn't going to hand it over to Doralina to buy Tang and cigarettes from the Kwik Stop.

When Theo wouldn't loan her money Doralina retaliated by creating fake problems in the house. One day when she came home from work Doralina was waiting for her, sitting somberly in the living room with her hands folded in her lap.

"Hello," Theo said, surprised to see her out of her ESPN cave.

"I have a problem," Doralina said gravely.

"Is your son okay?" Theo asked, her heart softening.

She worried for a second that he had been killed. Theo

had never met him; he lived with Doralina's mother, but each day as she walked in and out of the house she passed his picture. He looked about eight years old and smiled stiffly from behind the armor of his maroon-and-white school uniform. Doralina's mother had agreed to take care of him while she went back to school. But in the three months Theo had lived in the house she'd never seen Doralina do any schoolwork. In fact, the only time she ever left the house was when Theo gave her a ride somewhere.

Doralina looked confused for a second and said, "My son? He's fine."

"So what's the matter, then?"

She led Theo into the bathroom and pointed out some stray hairs trapped in a clump of suds in the bottom of the tub. Apparently, Doralina was pissed because Theo had been the last person to take a shower and four of her hairs were swimming in a small pool of water around the drain.

"We can't do that," Doralina said.

"This is the serious problem?" Theo asked.

Doralina glared at her.

"The drain sucks," Theo said. "I can't wait forty-five minutes after I'm done taking a shower for the tub to drain so then I can rinse it out. Otherwise I'd be late for *work*."

Theo spit out, *work*—the thing Doralina didn't do. She tried to convey her disgust for Doralina's joblessness by looking straight into her eyes with a martyr's gaze when she said the word *work*. Even the woman on *Hooked* who smoked twenty-five PCP cigarettes a day went to work—she in fact had *two* jobs, but Theo didn't say that.

Doralina returned Theo's cold stare and then repeated, "We can't do that," before angrily walking back to the kitchen, jerking her curtain to the side and going back into her cave.

Theo was desperate to find a job in Brooklyn, and at night after work she perused the get-rich-quick jobs on the back of the weekly newspaper. People were needed everywhere to donate their eggs, work on cruise ships and fishing boats, be in depression and alcohol studies. Most of all there were gentlemen looking for escorts. Theo picked up the phone and dialed Sammy.

"Tell me why I shouldn't get a job on a fishing boat?" Theo asked.

"Girl! It's cold and back-breaking and you will never get the fish smell off you. Never again."

"I can't live in this house another minute," Theo whispered.

"Good. Because I think I found us an apartment."

"Really?"

"Yeah, I'm just waiting for him to call back and make a time to see it. It's $695. One bedroom. Yard. In Sunset Park."

"They take dogs?"

"Yeah. The only bad thing is it's right next door to a car alarm store."

"How bad could that be?" Theo said glancing at the escort ads.

"Girl, are you there?" Sammy said after a short silence on the phone.

"Do you think I should be an escort or get into a depression study?"

Every queer Theo knew in San Francisco had done phone sex, been a dominatrix or a stripper or hooker.

"Oh, you're reading the back of the paper. Escort," Sammy said laughing. "It makes me think of Cary Grant in a top hat."

"Seriously. I have a wig," Theo said.

People could do anything if they put their mind to it, right? She hadn't had sex with a man since high school, but how hard could it really be?

"You're not really going to be a prostitute," Sammy said, a touch surprised.

"It can't hurt," Theo said. The dare of it filled her with courage. "I'll call you right back." She hung up and dialed the number of an escort agency.

"Hello," a woman answered after the first ring.

"Hello. I'm calling about the ad for the escort job," Theo said.

"Are you a police officer?"

Theo laughed.

The woman was silent.

"No," Theo quickly said.

"Have you escorted before?"

"No."

Theo could hear the woman hesitate so she added, "But my friends have. I know what the job is."

"Tell me what you look like," the woman said.

Theo knew not to tell her she was butch. Even though prostitution included special requests, she was sure there wasn't a great demand for timid sirma'amsirs.

"I'm five foot seven and a half inches. Brown eyes. A hundred and forty pounds."

"What's your bra size?" the woman interrupted.

"36 B," Theo lied.

Theo was flat as a board, even though she came from a long line of huge-breasted women. When she was ten she'd started to pray before bed *please God, don't give me any tits.* She'd been boyish for as long as she could remember, and when her chest remained flat while the chests of the girls on her soccer team grew, Theo wondered if she'd really saved herself with prayer.

"Well, there's a market for small-breasted women. What about tattoos? Do you have any?"

Theo was running out of truths the Madame could handle. Being a tattooed prostitute in San Francisco was a plus, but here in New York things were different.

"I have one," Theo started.

"What is it?"

Theo considered how to word it, and then just said, "A dagger?" as if she was asking permission.

She could hear the Madame's skepticism, "Where is the dagger?"

"On my chest, uh, between my breasts."

Theo was surprised to find herself invested in getting an escort interview. She was agitated by the woman's hesitation.

"How big is the dagger?"

"It's tasteful, I swear," Theo insisted.

"Can you come to the East Village around three o'clock tomorrow so I can take a look at you and see if you'd be the right fit for us?"

"Sure," Theo said, writing down the address.

⋮

Theo was too ashamed to tell anyone she'd gotten the idea for her first tattoo from a photograph in Madonna's *SEX* book. The picture was of Madonna sitting on the floor between two shaved-headed lesbians. Madonna, freshly emerged from a bondage scene, rubbing her rope-burned wrists. Theo didn't give a shit about Madonna having sex or getting tied up by lesbians. But she did care about the perfect dagger tattoo on one lesbian's chest, as if she'd swallowed the knife whole.

Theo had just broken up with Esther, her first girl-friend, but they were still doing everything together because even post-breakup they were committed to being *family*. On the bus to the tattoo shop Theo ran her fingers over the cross-hatched drawings in an ancient weaponry book she'd borrowed from the library. She liked how the ink on the cross-hatching sat raised on the page like a fingerprint. She was committed to two things for her first tattoo: It would be a dagger on her chest, and it wouldn't be wimpy. She remembered the fag bodybuilder who lived in her building and had the tiniest red rose tattooed on his rippling bicep. It was so small it looked like a sticker, or the design in the corner of a return address label. One day in the hallway they'd got to talking and Theo remembered him pointing to it and saying, "It was my first tattoo!" In that moment Theo decided, *I can never get a microscopic tattoo.* She would be tough, and her dagger would be a form of protection.

Many friends had recommended the tattoo artist, Gato. When Theo arrived for her appointment she handed him the ancient weaponry book and said, "I want a dagger on my chest."

Gato nodded, smirking, "A dagger for a dagger?"

Gato looked like a Hell's Angel, enormous with a shaved head and a neck covered in scary skull tattoos. Theo gave him a lukewarm smile, hoping he was gay. He flipped through the book asking Theo a multitude of questions about size and color and style, none of which Theo had thought about. The more questions Gato asked, the more confused she felt. She thought of the whole thing as an experience similar to losing your virginity; she'd been completely prepared to just lie down on the table and get up four hours later, tattooed, but more importantly, changed.

"Let me do some sketching and I'll show you what I come up with."

"Don't forget the filigree," Esther had said. "That's one of the things she really likes about those drawings."

Theo had grown weary of Esther's advocacy. Esther's only tattoo was a yin-yang symbol, the size of a quarter, on her ankle.

"I watched the tattoo artist tattoo for hours before I let her work on me," Esther had told Theo.

Gato wrote the word "filigree" down on a piece of tracing paper.

Theo and Esther sat in the waiting area drinking coffee until Gato appeared with a piece of tracing paper fluttering in his hand.

"Want to take a look?" he said.

Theo looked at the flurry of whirling pencil lines that somehow cohered into a dagger in Gato's mind.

"What do you think?" Gato asked, and then Esther joined in: "Do you like it?"

Theo had been hoping to see the same dagger she'd seen in Madonna's book, though she would never have asked for that.

"Well?" Esther prodded.

"Yeah," Theo said, even though it reminded her of some Dungeons and Dragons drawing or the cover of a fantasy novel. Theo hated the worlds and weaponries of wizards.

Gato pointed to the blade of the dagger and said, "I put in a lot of filigree here."

"Yeah," Theo said.

The worst part of the tattoo was the handle, where Gato

had drawn a sparkling round jewel. Theo hated the jewel, but she was terrified of Gato.

"I don't really want a jewel," she managed to say.

"You don't like the jewel?" he said, a touch defensively.

"You don't have to have the jewel," Esther chimed in.

"I just want it plain. No jewel," Theo said, her lower back sweating from asserting herself.

"That's easy enough," Gato said. "Give me five minutes to make some changes and then I'll show you what I've done."

When Gato was out of earshot at his drafting table Esther said, "If you don't like it, you don't have to get it today. He can redraw it."

"I like everything but the jewel," Theo lied.

Theo was not leaving without her tattoo, whether she liked the art or not.

"Take a look at this," Gato said, bright yellow pencil behind his ear, holding out the sketch.

Theo was surprised to see the jewel still there, sitting on top of the dagger. In fact, she couldn't figure out what was different about the drawing at all.

"I couldn't take out the jewel completely, because that would be weird—but I took out the lines that accented it. See, it's less jewel-y but it's still holding the place where the jewel should be."

This is how people end up buying new cars or timeshares, Theo thought. They're beaten down.

"That looks a lot better. A lot, a lot better," Theo said in a cheery voice she only used when depressed.

"Are you sure you like it?" Esther said. "Because, the jewel's still there."

"Yeah, I like it."

"Well, then come on back and we'll get started."

"Call me when you get home," Esther said, and left for work.

Theo felt relieved that Esther wouldn't be hovering over Gato's shoulder giving directions. She took off her shirt and lay down on the table self-consciously. She distracted herself by staring at Gato's artwork covering the walls. The subject matter seemed to consist solely of pin-up girls wearing strap-ons and holding space guns, bullwhips inserted in their asses.

"Here we go," Gato said, and Theo felt the needle go into her sternum where the horrible jewel lay at the tip of the dagger's handle.

"Tattoos always look different on the page than they do on the body," Gato said, and she wondered if he had picked up her fear about the jewel.

"So your first tattoo is a twelve-inch dagger, huh?" his voice held a hint of admiration.

Theo wanted to acknowledge him but she was afraid if she spoke he'd be able to hear the pain in her voice. It felt like someone was grating the skin off her sternum. He worked his way down the handle of the dagger to the blade, the tip ending right above her belly button. Theo was proud of herself for not being the kind of person who avoided getting a tattoo because it might hurt, but when Gato started inking her stomach the pain was excruciating and she gasped, feeling the needle dig into her guts.

"Do you want to take a break?" Gato sounded annoyed.

"I'm okay," she said. But in no time, when the tattoo gun resumed digging into her guts, she gasped again.

"If you need to take a break, just tell me," Gato said.

"Okay, maybe give me a minute."

One minute was exactly how much time he gave her before asking if she was ready to start again. He had bad vibes; exactly the kind of tattoo artist her friends had warned her against.

"You don't want someone to tattoo you who's going to be a dick," they'd said. "All their bad energy goes into you."

"Too late," Theo thought, holding in her pain for as long as she could before gasping again.

"You're going to make me fuck up if you keep breathing like that!"

So Theo made herself disappear—staring at Gato's tacky pin-up girl art until she finally heard the tattoo gun stop buzzing.

"Okay," he said. "The worst is over. Next visit will be a piece of cake."

Theo took a second to get up from the table. She was nauseous and her whole body was buzzing. Gato held up a hand mirror in front of her. The dagger that had once been on the piece of tracing paper was now permanently on her chest.

"Whoa," Theo said. "That's big."

"That's what twelve inches looks like," he sleazed.

When Theo got home she stared at her new tattoo in the mirror, from every possible angle. It was strange to see this new thing on her body. Did she like it? She applied lotion to it and slipped a V-neck T-shirt over her head, leaving only the handle of the dagger exposed. It looked too short. She looked harder into the mirror and her heart sank. She realized that with only the handle of the dagger emerging from the V-neck it looked like she had a penis tattooed on her chest. The jewel that Theo had thought too Dungeons and Dragons now looked like the tip of a penis, complete with piss hole. The harder she looked the more horrors she noticed: coursing veins running down the shaft. Theo turned off the light in the bathroom and walked numbly into the living room to call Esther.

"Can you come over?" Theo asked.

"Are you okay?"

"Just come over."

Over the next two weeks when Theo showed her dick tattoo to friends, some suggested Gato had done it on purpose because he was an asshole or misogynist or because Esther had nagged him about the filigree. Worse still, maybe he was a soldier in some sort of secret misogyny militia tattooing dicks on queer women across America. But Theo put all her hope into her next visit, when Gato could correct the problem.

When she arrived he asked her how she was getting used to her new tattoo.

She immediately betrayed herself. "Fine."

"Tell him, tell him," her mind said.

He'd been tattooing a few minutes before she got her courage up.

"Um," she started, "I was wondering if you could do anything to fix the handle of the dagger. It kind of looks like a dick."

He stopped tattooing and looked at her.

"You think it looks like a dick?" he laughed.

Theo had never expected him to dispute it.

"It does look like a dick," Theo said. "Everyone thinks so."

"I wouldn't say it looks like a dick," he said. "Maybe a cigar."

Theo looked at his horrible face.

"Can you do anything," she asked, "to de-dickify it?"

"Once all the shading is down I don't think it'll look like a dick."

A little while later Gato said, "Okay, you're all done!" and handed Theo a mirror.

She took a deep breath before looking. *Please God,* she thought, *don't let it be a dick.*

When she opened her eyes the dick was still there except now the veins and piss hole were shaded in perfect 3-D.

"How's that?" Gato said. "Do you like it?"

⋮

Theo felt a touch guilty calling in sick to her data entry job in order to go to the escort interview. She had nothing to wear, so she waited for Megan to leave for her job at the bank and then snuck into the rabbit hoarder's room, rummaging around in her dresser until she found a pair of ruffled peach panties. Theo put them on, thinking *now my pussy has touched her pussy.* Doralina's TV was already on, giving sports recaps from the day before. Theo prayed she wouldn't come upstairs and catch her cross-dressing in Megan's room. She scowled at the wallfull of rabbits in cages, warning them into silence.

Once she secured the panties, Theo sifted through the makeup on Megan's bureau. She knew enough to know that it was all cheap drugstore stuff. If it wasn't three hours earlier in San Francisco and Olivia didn't sleep until noon, Theo could call and find out exactly what color eye shadow a person should wear to an escort interview. Instead, she put on bright blue, with hot pink lipstick, and completed her conversion by hiding her Marine haircut under the Butch Bathroom Wig. With the wig, panties, and drugstore makeup, Theo wore her regular clothes— jeans and a hoodie and her pair of busted black Converse hi-tops. She snuck out of the house with Cary Grant and drove to the Kwik Stop to get a cup of coffee.

Theo was surprised to see a news crew interviewing Randy in the parking lot. She waved to him, but he didn't wave back. She went in and poured herself a coffee.

"Hi," she said to Randy who came in and stared at her blankly. "It's Theo!"

"Why do you look like that?" he said.

"I'm going on an interview. What's up with the news crew?"

"Someone bought a winning lottery ticket here but hasn't claimed the prize yet. It's over three million dollars."

"No!" Theo gasped.

Randy nodded.

"Three million dollars," Theo said.

She put her coffee on the counter to pay, feeling something bubble up inside her.

"Let me get five of those," she pointed to a lottery scratch-off ticket called *Dog-Gone Riches*.

"That's not the kind she won on. It was a quick pick."

Theo held out her twenty-dollar bill until he took it.

"Coffee is on the house," Randy said, ringing her up for the lottery tickets. "Come hang out with me." He tapped the milk crate behind the counter.

"I can't," Theo lied. "I have my interview."

"For what kind of job?"

She started scratching the metallic dog bones off.

"What if I won fifty thousand dollars right now?" she asked Randy.

"Is that the top prize?"

Theo nodded. She scratched all of the dog bones off and double-checked she hadn't won anything.

"Fuck."

"What kind of job?" Randy repeated.

"Oh. Receptionist. That's why I have the wig and make up. To look professional."

"But it's okay if you wear jeans?" Randy asked sweetly looking at her Levis.

"Well, I was going to go to a thrift store in the city before my interview and try to find some woman clothes. I'll let you know what happens."

"Look for me on the news tonight," Randy said as she walked out.

Theo didn't want to drive to the city in rush-hour traffic so she stopped at a donut shop for an apple fritter. She had enough money for eight more *Dog-Gone Riches* scratch-off tickets, a coffee and the apple fritter. From her table she could see Cary Grant looking out the truck window. She left the lottery tickets unscratched while she ate her donut. She had a feeling they were more duds and didn't want to rush finding out she was unlucky. As long as the tickets sat beside her unscratched, the possibility remained that she could become instantly rich and not need to find a job. She ate her donut waiting for someone to bust her, call her out on her costume, but no one was paying attention. They were chain-smoking or reading or doing crosswords or clipping their fingernails and letting them drop onto the floor, a practice Theo found harrowing to watch.

Her lipstick had gotten smeared with the first bite of apple fritter. Her attitude about becoming a prostitute, so cavalier last night, had become a nervous dread. She hadn't even had sex with a man since high school, what was she thinking? She could be murdered, she thought, even though none of her friends had ever been murdered working as prostitutes. They'd made it seem as easy as returning a video, but they weren't butches. Theo dreaded undressing in front of the madam, trying to explain her dagger tattoo.

When she was first coming to terms with the penis on her chest, her friends suggested she turn lemons into lemonade: "Use it as a pick-up line. You can pull down the collar of your shirt and say, 'Hey wanna suck my dick?'"

Theo finished her donut but was afraid to move the wig hairs out of her face because her fingertips were covered in donut glaze. She pulled a quarter from her pocket and began scratching the first ticket. *If I win*, she told herself, *I will not go to the interview.* She began scratching the metallic dog bones. If she revealed three of the same amount, that's what she would win. She won nothing on the first ticket. On the second, she almost won $50,000, getting two out of three necessary. But in the end it amounted to nothing. She continued scratching the rest of the tickets, hoping the jackpot would be revealed in the last ticket the way such fortunes reversed in old stories, but the last ticket gave her nothing either. She'd wasted almost twenty dollars. She dropped the losing tickets in the trash can and walked out of the donut shop, the cold wind hitting her face, blowing long strands of the wig into the corners of her mouth and eyes. She wasn't used to having long hair and she felt like she'd walked face-first into a spider web. Cary Grant pawed at Theo when she sat down in the driver's seat, and she decided to drive to Brooklyn to see Sammy.

The inside of the truck was toasty and Theo rested her hand on the dog's back as she drove. Her plan was to show up on Sammy's doorstep in her escort interview costume and ask her if she looked like a believable prostitute. When she got to the cluster of apartment buildings she couldn't remember which one was Sammy's so she called her from the pay phone downstairs. It was 10 AM.

"Sammy?"

"Yeah." She sounded like she'd just woken up.

"It's Theo."

"Hey."

"I'm downstairs," Theo said.

"At my place?"

"Yeah. Where the pay phones are."

"Why?"

"I called in sick from my data entry job so I could interview to be an escort."

"I'll be right down."

Theo wrapped her arms around Cary Grant, who was shivering, and waited for Sammy to come downstairs.

"Do you need a winter sweater?" she said to the dog, who kept shying away from the wig. Cary Grant started to wag, and Theo turned to see Sammy coming toward them.

"Cary Grant," Sammy said and the dog's ears went back, waiting to be petted. "You look insane," she said to Theo.

"Really?"

"Uh, yes. But I have good news. Remember that apartment I was telling you about for $695? The one-bedroom in Sunset Park?"

Theo nodded.

"You want to go look at it? The landlord said he was going to be there this morning until noon, working on it."

"What about my interview?" Theo asked, certain now that she was too chicken to go.

Sammy just stared at her like she was some kind of impossible math problem. They got in the truck and drove to the address Sammy had written down. Theo parked a few blocks away so she could take off her wig and makeup. They left Cary Grant in the truck and walked down 4th Avenue under the giant green BQE overpass, adult video stores peppered in between bodegas. With each step, Theo's hopes were dashed a little more. The humble little apartment she'd imagined when driving cross-country was surely not inside the house that matched the address Sammy had on a slip of paper.

"What do you think, girl?" Sammy asked.

They sensed each other's apprehension and stood staring at the three-family house with peeling green paint. Theo tried to find the word for what was wrong with it. *Soulless,* which was strange because how could a dilapidated house where so many people lived be without a soul? Usually soulless was for new, sterile apartment buildings built for the unimaginative dweller. To the left of the house was a car alarm store, and across the street a graffiti-covered Muslim Elementary School.

"Maybe the inside's good," Theo said.

In fact, it didn't matter if the inside was good or not; Theo desperately needed to get out of Yonkers. She followed Sammy's gaze down the peopleless street where many of the houses were covered in Christmas lights and Puerto Rican flags. It felt like an early Sunday morning but it was a weekday close to noon, and even though the sun was out it seemed to shine sadly.

Sammy opened the gate in the chain-link fence and rang the doorbell of the first-floor apartment. Behind her, a light wind made tiny cyclones of garbage swirl in the driveway, occasionally pushing them flat against the fence. Theo watched a prostitute come around the corner with a bag of plantain chips and a soda. She'd once heard someone say that intersections under overpasses are major hooker corners, because guys who like $5 blowjobs also like to get right back on the highway.

When no one came to the door Sammy shrugged her shoulders at Theo and came back out to where she was smoking and shifting from foot to foot to keep warm.

"I need boots," Theo said. "And a coat."

Just then a gray sedan screeched to the curb in front of the house and a middle-aged Hasidic man popped out of the car, walking toward them in a rush and giving each a weak handshake. He fished through a bunch of keys on a ring.

"I'm Abraham," he said.

They followed him to the metal front door and Theo watched over his shoulder as he tried the same key in four different deadbolts. Theo presumed the fresh coat of shiny green paint was an effort to try and cover the obvious pry marks from where someone had tried to break in. Once inside, Abraham pulled on a chain hanging from a lightbulb a few times before giving up and leading them down a dark hallway to a second door. Theo tried to inconspicuously point out the glut of mousetraps lining the baseboards to Sammy. Finally, Abraham got the second door open and they entered the apartment through the living room. The walls were painted the brightest white, but even though it was on the first floor it had the darkness of a basement apartment because of a second-floor window that protruded over the driveway. Some thin stripes of light filtered through the bars over the two front windows and fell across an expanse of thin brown linoleum that rippled across the living room, the corners curling up. Theo and Sammy walked over the wavy linoleum, following Abraham into the enormous kitchen.

The kitchen floor was covered with drop cloths and paint pans. In the sink were plastic bags filled with hardware store purchases: roach spray, mousetraps, tubes of synthetic caulking. On the far wall was an indentation that looked like it had once been a small window, but was now boarded up and painted over. Whoever had cleaned the apartment had forgotten the mustard-yellow hood over the stove, which had a pelt of gray grease covered in dust bunnies. Theo stopped trying to gauge Sammy's expression and walked into a bedroom off the kitchen that was covered in the same linoleum as the living room. It was big enough for a bed and a dresser and had a barred window the size of a pizza box, set abnormally high up on the wall. Through the pizza-box window, Theo could see the gray limbs of a leafless tree reaching toward the sky.

Theo and Sammy followed Abraham into the long, narrow, bathroom where next to an ancient radiator was a toilet whose base was held together with foam caulking. A bathtub the exact same color as the grease-covered range hood sat across from the sink and ancient medicine cabinet. At the end of the bathroom was a steel fire door with a long metal latch that Abraham said led to the backyard. He slid the latch to open the door, making a horrible screech of metal on metal.

The backyard was a long, narrow plot of dirt bordered on one side by the brick wall of the car alarm store and on the other by a falling-down chain-link fence. In the middle of the yard was the tree Theo had seen from the bedroom window. She didn't know trees, but if she were on a game show she'd guess *cherry tree*. Against its gray trunk rested discarded metal fencing, scrap metal and chunks of broken cement. Abraham stood on a cracked concrete patio, complete with crumbling cement barbecue, right off the bathroom door. He looked like someone being interviewed on the news in a war-torn or earthquake-ruined country. Theo took in the pieces of rusting metal, children's shoes and empty dishwashing liquid bottles around the base of the barbeque.

"We're still fixing it up." Abraham said, "The old tenant just moved out and she'd lived here for quite a while. But you get the picture."

They did get the picture. The picture was like a dream in which someone tries to convince you that the things you're seeing really are those things that you want to see. This is the thing called "a backyard" that you want to have so you can give your dog the thing called "happiness," and the whole time in the dream you walk around saying, "but this doesn't seem like a backyard" and "this doesn't seem like happiness."

Sammy and Theo exchanged skeptical glances.

"Are you still working on the backyard, too?" Theo asked Abraham, who didn't seem to see the backyard as a garbage dump.

He didn't say anything, so Theo continued, "Like, is all this garbage still going to be here?"

"Well, I can ask my handyman to clean this up a bit."

The way he answered made Theo feel as if she was wrong for asking. Sammy's face reflected what Theo felt: Of course she didn't want this shit hole but they would be forced to take it because this is where people like them could afford to live. Abraham fiddled with his enormous ring of jangling keys.

"What do you think, girl?" Theo asked. "Do you want to take it?"

"Whatever you want," Sammy said.

Theo thought of Yonkers and Doralina and Megan's stolen underwear and said, "Okay, we'll take it."

Abraham said he only needed a check for the first month's rent and deposit and it was a deal.

"I don't really have any money on me," Theo said, fingering the four dollars she had left after buying the lottery tickets.

"You can pay me back," Sammy said, pulling out her wad of fishing boat cash. She counted out $1,400 in hundred-dollar bills and asked Abraham for a receipt, which he wrote out bent over the hood of his car.

"You can come back Friday when the work's done and I'll give you the keys then," he said. They watched his gray sedan screech off.

"Girl?" Sammy said.

"That fucking backyard," Theo said.

"There are children buried back there, for sure," Sammy said. "But we can fix it up—get a picnic table and some lawn chairs."

The farther they got away from the apartment the better they felt.

"We'll make it nice," Sammy said. "We'll drive over the Verazzano Bridge and go to IKEA."

⋮

Theo was determined to pay Sammy back as soon as possible; she wasn't used to letting anyone pay her way. She couldn't believe Sammy was going to be her roommate. They only knew each other from that short time in jail, but Sammy already felt like a long-lost sibling. They were both going to start new life chapters—Sammy in massage school and Theo in *real* New York.

The next day Theo went to the Kwik Stop before work to get a cup of coffee.

"Did you see me on TV?" Randy asked. He was putting up Christmas decorations in the windows.

"Oh," Theo said. "I forgot to watch."

He looked disappointed.

"The person with the winning ticket still hasn't come forward," Randy said.

"Really?"

Theo's stomach dropped. She imagined the winner somewhere working as a fast-food employee, covered in fry grease, oblivious to the fact that they were a millionaire.

"Maybe they lost it," Randy said, setting down his decorations on a milk crate.

"That's so depressing," Theo said, pausing. And then, "Guess what? I'm moving to Brooklyn."

She tried to keep her voice from sounding too excited. During the three months she'd been in Yonkers she'd made a point to visit him while he was working. The backbone of their friendship was that they were both miserable in Yonkers.

"Really?"

His eyes looked disappointed. For a split second, Theo thought about saying, "You can come too," but she stopped herself.

"You'll have to come down and spend the night some time," she said, but she didn't know how Randy would fit into her new life.

"But I work every day," he whined.

Theo could see she'd hurt him.

"Well, on your next day off." She wanted to change the subject. "Do you have any empty boxes I could use to pack my room?"

He nodded. "They're next to the dumpster out back."

She was anxious to get away from his sad-sack energy.

"When do you move into your new place?" Randy asked.

"Friday."

"Will you come see me before you go?"

"Of course," Theo said, "but let me hug you now just in case."

She leaned forward to hug Randy's thin body and as she did, she knew this would be their good-bye, because she couldn't bear to see his disappointed face again.

It was cold outside as she scooped up the flattened boxes and put them in the back of her truck. Theo still hadn't bought herself a winter coat or warm shoes, though she'd bought a gray-and-lavender argyle turtleneck dog sweater that made Cary Grant look even more dapper, if that was possible.

When Theo got home from work Doralina and Megan were lying on Megan's bed playing with one of the rabbits. Theo stopped in the doorway with the cardboard boxes folded under her arm.

"I found a place to live in Brooklyn," she burst out, eyeing the rabbit.

Doralina looked stunned.

"When?"

"Friday."

"Well, I need thirty days' notice."

Theo hadn't signed a lease, and now that she had a new plan for life she didn't care what Doralina thought.

"So let's count from now," she said. "Today is day one."

Theo went into her room with the boxes and could hear them whispering for a long time. She had no plan to pay rent for the next thirty days, so she figured she could kiss her deposit good-bye.

⋮

Theo got up early Friday morning to shuttle all her posses-sions into her truck. She wanted to drive directly to the new apartment after work.

She arrived earlier than normal to the data entry of-fice and went straight to the lounge to start a pot of coffee; her stomach was a mix of nervousness and excitement. Her whole life she'd been afraid when it was time to quit a job—even those she hated.

"You don't have to do that," Mimi said, seeing Theo fill the coffeepot with water. She leaned down and gave Cary Grant a scritch.

"Oh, this sweater is too much!" Mimi said, fiddling with the dog's turtleneck collar.

"I'm quitting today," Theo blurted out, not wanting to hold onto a secret.

"What?" Mimi's face tightened and she looked like she was about to get mean.

With all of Theo's fuck-ups, she'd still always given two weeks' notice. But Yonkers felt like some kind of infection that she had to get rid of.

"I don't really want to get into it, but I have a family emergency," Theo lied. "I'm moving to Brooklyn today after work."

"I didn't know you had family in Brooklyn."

Theo nodded, giving the "exasperated family look" and then changed the subject.

"When should I tell Joseph? At the beginning or end of the day?"

"Either way he's going to be pissed. I mean we just fi-nally got you trained," Mimi said, walking away.

Theo felt a sense of shame wash over her, like she'd dis-appointed her family. *Am I fucking up my life by quitting this job before I have another one?* Her head was muddled. When the coffee was done she went into her office to pretend to work. The tiny window that connected her office to Joseph's was dim. He wasn't in yet. She collected some faxes, arranged them on her desk neatly, lit a cigarette and dialed Sammy's number from her desk phone. No one answered. Theo began to type up the faxes, waiting for her favorite vendor to come by with donuts. When she looked down again she realized she'd drained her cup of coffee and finished her cigarette. She crushed it out, disgusted by the smell of its burning filter.

At noon, when Joseph still hadn't arrived, Mimi came and stood in the doorway to Theo's office.

"You're off the hook," she said. "He's sick."

"Well, how should I tell him I'm quitting? Should I leave him a note?"

"I told him over the phone."

"You did? Was he mad?"

"Not at all, actually. He told me to wish you luck with your family situation and to make sure to use us as a reference."

"Really?" Theo asked. She felt guilty. Maybe her luck was changing.

"Deep down he's a softie. Well, I'm going to miss you guys," Mimi said. She was staring at Cary Grant, who was lying next to Theo's desk, dreaming of running. Her paws flipped back and forth on the blanket, making Mimi smile. "If you want to work a half day, I won't tell. I can write you your last check now," she said.

"That would be really helpful," Theo said, alluding to her fake family emergency. Sometimes it scared Theo how easily she could lie.

When Mimi left, she dialed Sammy, "I'm leaving work early."

"Perfect, because Abraham said to meet us at the apartment in an hour for keys and a walk-through."

Theo gathered Cary Grant's things, retrieved her last check and gave Mimi an awkward hug good-bye. Outside it was cold, the sky a light gray, as if the sun was a faraway frozen marble. She sat in the truck with the engine idling while she waited for the heater to stop blowing cold air and draped a sweatshirt over Cary Grant, who was already wearing the sweater.

Sammy was inside with Abraham when Theo arrived. In the few days since they'd first seen the apartment Theo had improved it in her mind. Now that she saw it was still a piece of shit, her heart sank a little. She stared at the brown linoleum rolling across the living room floor in waves.

"Aren't you going to tack this down?" Sammy asked Abraham, who pretended nothing was wrong with the floor.

"Do you see how it's wavy? And bumpy?"

Sammy grabbed a corner of the linoleum and peeled back half the living room floor. Underneath were piles of crayons and coffee-stained napkins. Sammy refused to move until Abraham made eye contact with one of the piles of broken crayons. When he did, they filed into the large kitchen whose baseboards were lined with roach strips and mousetraps. Sammy put her foot into the space between the oven and the wall and sent skidding across the floor an old trap complete with dead mouse. Theo looked away, afraid to see Abraham's expression, and found herself looking straight at the filthy range hood, dust bunnies trapped in the grease; it looked like some kind of avant-garde taxidermy.

Abraham hadn't said a word, fiddling with his beeper. Theo didn't want to live in a shit hole but was scared Abraham would take the apartment back if Sammy kept asserting herself.

In the bedroom, Sammy tried to flip on the light switch to no avail.

"So we have the linoleum, the bedroom light switch, the dead mouse," Sammy said, keeping the list for Abraham, who'd stuffed his hands inside his pockets and wasn't writing anything down. Then they all walked to the backyard through the bathroom with the sullen posture of a family holding onto a terrible secret.

When Theo had first seen the backyard, it had struck her as the kind of place that ends up on the news. She imagined being interviewed by the police: "I was just raking some of the leaves when I saw what looked like a femur. I guess I always thought the yard was a little creepy."

"I thought this garbage was going to be hauled out," Sammy said, pointing to the pile of empty soap bottles and childrens' shoes.

"Let me call my handyman, and you can talk to him about it," Abraham said, as though the problem were between Theo and Sammy and the handyman.

"Girl!" Sammy said, when Abraham walked to the corner pay phone to call the handyman.

"Girl," Theo said back. "What the fuck?"

Abraham returned twenty minutes later with Andy the handyman. Andy's emaciated drug-addict physique was accentuated by the belt that wrapped around his tiny waist and was clipped full of pagers.

"So what's the problem?" Andy said, slurping the top off a lemon ice inside a Dixie cup.

Theo let out a laugh, and everyone looked at her.

"How come there are crayons under the linoleum?" Theo heard herself say.

"And dirty napkins," Sammy said.

Andy kicked the crayons out of the way with the toe of his sneaker and then folded the piece of linoleum back across the floor, smoothing one corner down like he was sealing an envelope. Then he slurped some more of his lemon ice and took a step back as if he was getting perspective on a painting he was creating. They all looked at the bumps that still remained.

"See how it's wavy," Sammy said.

They were all actors in an absurdist play.

"It just needs to stretch out," Andy said. "It's like new leather right now and it hasn't had time to relax."

Theo and Sammy watched him finish the lemon ice and then crumple the Dixie cup in his hand.

"I don't think linoleum is like leather," Sammy said.

In the bedroom Sammy stood in front of the light switch, flipping it on and off with no result.

"Do you have a screwdriver?" Andy asked Sammy.

Theo had never met a handyman who had no tools.

She stared at him while Abraham jingled the change in his pocket. Then Andy threw his crinkled Dixie cup on the bedroom floor and pulled a nail clipper out of his pocket. He pulled out the file and used it to take the little screw out of the light switch plate, which fell off the wall.

"Whoaaa," Andy said. "Come take a look at this."

They watched as he prodded at something in the wall with the tip of the nail file. There was a quick crinkling sound.

"See this," Andy said. "See all this," he pointed the nail file, and each time he prodded it let out another crinkle.

Theo didn't know what he was pointing at.

"All these are roach bodies," he said touching the brown papery bodies with the file. "The electricity can't make a connection because there's too many in the wall."

"Okay," Sammy said. "We're going to come back in half an hour and we want all the garbage out of the back yard and the light switch fixed and the linoleum tacked down."

"Oh yeah, no problem," Andy said.

Sammy took the keys from Abraham on the way out and they got into Theo's truck, where Cary Grant was sleeping. Theo lit a cigarette and looked at Sammy.

"Girl," Sammy said.

"Andy is going to fix everything thing," Theo replied.

"Andy the handyman."

"The Andyman."

They both laughed.

"I've never met a handyman without a screwdriver," Sammy said.

"What about when he threw his cup on the ground?"

Neither Sammy nor Theo brought up the death camp of roaches unearthed in the wall.

"Let's go to the check-cashing place so I can cash my last check," Theo said.

Sammy nodded. "And we'll go to the 99-Cent store and get a bunch of cleaning supplies. But I have to smoke a joint first."

six

Theo and Sammy were determined to make their new apartment a nice home. Theo swept up the roach bodies and the crayons and Andy's lemon ice cup while Sammy unpacked their IKEA purchases. Sammy sat in the living room assembling the entertainment center while Theo scrubbed the bathroom floor, trying to coax an unwilling Cary Grant into the backyard. Each time Theo opened the door, the dog looked shyly into the yard and then ran back to the edge of the futon.

One of the few things Theo had moved from San Francisco was large piece of blue fabric with yellow sunflowers on it. While they weren't exactly Van Gogh's sunflowers, Theo had bought it with him in mind. She cut the fabric into two equal pieces and nailed them over the front windows for curtains. She also had black-and-white newspaper photos of two of Van Gogh's paintings; one was his sunflowers, and the other, the famous picture of his boots. She taped them on the wall between the front windows, and Sammy hung a Cary Grant poster over the bed. When she'd finally finished assembling the shaky entertainment center, she placed her TV and boom box on it, leaving the top shelf for some tea lights and a paint can that she used to collect loose change.

Instead of a kitchen table, Sammy installed her most prized possession—a tall plywood bar, painted in 1970s puke-yellow, with two matching vinyl barstools. Theo and Sammy would eat their cereal there while resting their forearms on the cushioned armrest designed for the weary elbows of hardcore drinkers. Whenever Sammy collected enough change in her paint can she'd take it to the Coinstar machine and use the money to buy an enormous bottle of liquor to stock the bar. For years, she told Theo, she'd been slowly filling the bar's empty shelves with every kind of alcohol, even liquors she didn't drink. She'd worked for many years as a bartender, and she didn't like the idea of not being able to serve a friend exactly the drink they wanted.

"We could run a bar out of the house for extra money," Sammy said. "Like a neighborhood place. Did you ever see John Waters on that late night talk show, talking about the bar he went to in Baltimore? It could be like that."

John Waters had said how everyone knew this woman who had a bar in her house, and you could ring the doorbell and, no matter what time it was, she would answer the door, often in her bathrobe, head full of rollers, and invite you into her house and make you a drink. He said he'd had a wonderful time; they sat together, her in her bathrobe and bunny slippers, him in his plaid suit, and she'd served him his drink and sat next to him while he drank it.

"We could do that," Sammy said.

Theo listened, trying to identify what she was feeling, adrenaline or hope; either way it was good.

"The only bummer would be if we were tired and didn't want to get up at 3 AM," Theo said.

"We could have a code. Like a red lightbulb outside the door," Sammy said. "We would only be open for business if people saw the red light on."

Theo considered the fact that earlier in the day they hadn't been able to get even one lightbulb turned on due to the quantity of roach bodies in the wall, and that anyone who would be coming to their apartment bar for a drink at 3 AM might not be someone they wanted to let in.

"What if it's not people like John Waters that come?" she asked Sammy. "What if they're alcoholics? It won't matter if the red lightbulb is on or not. They'll just keep ringing."

"We'll know them. They'll be our friends. We'll be the kind of bar that gives waitresses and strippers their first drink free," Sammy said formulating her business plan.

"What will you call the bar?" Theo asked.

"Cary's!"

Theo smiled at the dog sleeping on the futon. She wondered if the Andyman would ever show up at 3 AM wanting to trade empty lemon ice cups for a drink.

⋮

Now that Theo had an apartment she needed to get a job so she could pay Sammy back. She'd always had a job. A job made her feel grounded, even if she hated it. Maybe it was the hatred that grounded her. She also needed a library card, a haircut and a new pair of shoes. With these she felt she could survive anything.

The wad of mostly fives and ones from her last data entry check was fat in her pocket. After a few hours of walking up and down 4th Avenue with Cary Grant looking for HELP WANTED signs she decided she felt rich enough to buy herself a slice of pizza. She sat on a fire hydrant eating the slice, feeding a big piece of crust to Cary Grant.

The dog chewed the crust slowly. Theo sat on the fire hydrant people-watching. She loved New York. It was *authentic*. The energy in New York was different from anywhere else she'd ever been—it was everywhere, like a blanket that she wanted to rub her face in. She felt it mostly on public transportation, getting on and off of the subways, traveling up the staircase with a herd of people, and she loved it. It felt like hope.

Theo finally got up, and Cary Grant, who still had a slight limp, walked beside her in her new argyle sweater. The dog had adjusted well to her new life, but Theo had become familiar with all of her movements and was starting to notice tiny nuances. The dog's face got nervous if she had to pass through too many people on the sidewalk, and when Theo noticed the tightened brow, she'd bend down and comfort Cary Grant, patting her.

They walked for blocks, until Theo came upon a bunch of old men leaning against a wall, smoking. The sign said OTB, Off Track Betting. Inside it was filled with packs of men pacing and spitting and studying the horses who ran in tight ovals on the TVs. The floor was covered in white receipts, scraps of newspaper and sunflower seed shells. Then suddenly, as if some kind of work whistle had gone off, the herd of men outside crushed their cigarettes and filed inside with their newspapers folded under their arms. Theo looped Cary Grant's leash around a newspaper stand and followed them, the gambling demon waking up inside her. With the exception of herself and a middle-aged dyke working one of the cashier windows, it seemed like everyone in the room was an elderly man. She scanned the place until she spotted a guy who looked like he was in his early twenties. He was wearing a backwards baseball cap with the Puerto Rican flag on it. Theo walked over to him.

"Hi," she said.

"Hey."

"I've never bet horses before," Theo started. "How does this work?"

He pointed to the TV, where jockeys were leading their horses around the track. "You pick the horse you want and then you can pick whether you think it's going to win, place or show. Or you can pick a couple horses."

Theo looked at the television; horses' names were listed with their jockeys and the odds of them winning the race.

"These races are already over," he said, showing her a newspaper where he'd circled names with a pen: There were three horses with 1, 2, and 3 written next to them. "I usually bet trifecta. You can win a lot more money because the odds are so much greater. See, I'm betting that these three horses are going to finish first, second, and third."

He held his newspaper up to Theo to see if she was getting it.

"You could just bet two dollars if you wanted," he said. "Say you just want to bet the long shot."

Theo pulled a bill off the wad of money in her pocket. "Would you put this on the long shot for me?" Theo asked. She didn't realize it was a twenty until it was too late.

"You like the long shot, huh?"

"I like an underdog," Theo said.

"Well, sometimes they win. And then you can make a lot of money."

He looked at the paper and pointed, "Buttermilk is the long shot. 255 to 1. I'll be right back."

He stood in line where the dyke was working and when it was his turn slipped the twenty dollars through the small opening. He handed Theo a slip of paper when he came back and stood next to her.

"Thanks," she said as she took it. "I'm Theo."

"Big Vic," he smiled.

Theo saw he was missing a tooth.

"My real name's Victor," he said.

"Okay, Big Vic. Let's win this thing."

They turned back to the television, where the horses had just left the gate. Big Vic had bet on the front-runners, but as a gesture to Theo had also put two dollars on Buttermilk to win. By the time the horses had made it around the first curve of the track, the entire roomful of old men had become impassioned, shouting at the television in a multitude of languages.

"Come on," Big Vic yelled, a touch of anger in his voice.

Theo had lost track of Buttermilk in the sea of horses, and then as quickly as the race had started, it ended—with most of the old men throwing their tickets on the ground and a few walking up to the cashier windows. Their gestures and body language seemed over the top, as if they were a bunch of movie set extras vying for the role of losing gamblers.

"Well?" Theo said.

"Uh, you just won a lot of money," Big Vic said slapping Theo twice in the arm.

"How much?"

"Let's go see."

They brought their tickets to the cashier window. The room was almost empty and most of the old men had returned outside to smoke. The dyke took Big Vic's ticket and slid a pile of cash to him through the hole in the bottom of the window. Then she took Theo's ticket and exclaimed, "Nice!"

Theo watched her grab a bundle of hundred-dollar bills and count out fifty-one.

"You want an envelope?" the cashier asked.

"Yes," Theo said, nodding. Her heart was pounding against her chest.

"That's five grand," Big Vic said in a low voice.

The cashier handed Theo an envelope thick with hundred-dollar bills, and Theo took one out and gave it to Big Vic before folding the envelope in half and shoving it in her pocket.

"This is for helping me," Theo said.

"No way," he said trying to refuse it.

"Please," Theo said, and he took it.

"How did you know to bet on that horse?" Big Vic asked.

"I just had a feeling. Did you hear about that person in Yonkers who won three million dollars playing Lotto but never claimed it?"

"Yeah."

"I worked at the store that sold the ticket. Anyway, I just had a feeling about Buttermilk."

"I'm glad I put some money down, too. Otherwise I would've been pissed."

Big Vic looked at the clock.

"I gotta take off for work. But maybe I'll see you. I come here all the time."

"Yeah," Theo said. "See you."

Theo had forgotten she'd left Cary Grant tied to the newspaper stand, and she found the dog shivering and looking for her nervously. She put one hand on each side of the dog and kissed the top of her head repeatedly.

"I'm so sorry," she whispered into the dog's cold ears.

Theo was dying to tell Sammy she'd won money on the horses, but when she got home the apartment was empty. She counted out the seven hundred dollars she owed Sammy and put it on top of the bar under a bottle of Campari. Then she peeled off three hundred dollars for herself and hid the rest in her coffee can.

The next order of business was to buy herself a pair of winter boots. She returned to 4th Avenue excited, wondering if she only had to think positively in order to make things happen. How had she known Buttermilk would win? Could people really make anything come true with positive thinking? Now she wanted to manifest the perfect pair of work boots. She'd heard a long time ago, "Shoes make the man." She bet they made the sirma'amsir, too. Ten years ago a roommate had given her a perfectly worn pair of leather ankle boots. She'd had them resoled until they were completely destroyed. Now, as she walked down 4th Avenue, Theo looked in every window for a pair of boots like the kind Van Gogh had painted. Eventually, she stumbled upon an old-timey menswear store.

She walked in and was immediately hit with a wall of musty air. The store was a sirma'amsir's dream come true, with classic pajama sets like the real Cary Grant would wear, folded neatly over pieces of square cardboard and wrapped in plastic. An old, white-haired black man sat on a stool behind the counter next to a space heater, reading the *New York Post*. Theo nodded hello, then wandered to the wall where a variety of dusty sample boots sat on top of their boxes. It was a whole store of dead stock—straight from the 1950s.

She wouldn't have been surprised to find Van Gogh's boots among the ones on the wall. She scanned the available sizes of black leather ankle boots with silver eyelets until she found an 8½ men's. She slid the box out, careful not to topple the tower of boxes above it, and unwrapped thin paper from the boots.

"You find what you're looking for?" the old man yelled over to her.

"Yes," Theo said.

"Okay," he said, turning the page of the newspaper.

Theo unlaced her busted black Converse and looked at the toenail on her big toe pushing through her thin sock. Now that her feet were out of the shoes she realized they were numb and freezing. It had always been hard for her to buy herself socks, and hard to throw away socks that were rendered useless. She didn't know why. She didn't think twice about putting twenty dollars on the long shot, and she had no problem buying Cary Grant a forty-dollar sweater. She slipped her feet into the stiff leather boots, tied them, and took a few steps so she could get a look at them in the mirror. They were so perfect she wanted to cry; she felt like a house with a new foundation. She put her old Converse in the box and carried it up to the counter where the old man laid his newspaper down.

"All set?" he said.

"I'm gonna wear them home," Theo told him.

"All right, then," he said, adding, "You need anything else? Socks? Drawers?"

Theo loved that the old man called underwear "drawers." He was reading her as a man; when he said, "drawers?" he'd held up a three-pack of plain white boxer shorts.

"I'll get some socks," Theo said.

She looked at the variety on the counter, feeling the cushioning in the foot and heel, and settled on a three-pack of plain white ones. The old man wrote down the price of the socks and boots on a pad of paper, and got out a calculator to figure the tax. She paid him, imagining how good her feet would feel in those cushiony new socks.

"You want to keep these?" the old man said referring to Theo's old Converse.

Theo knew she should say no, but she would put them on the street for someone. She'd always been like that—one pair in, one pair out. The old man wrapped her old shoes carefully, as if they were new, folding the tissue around each one, then closing the box gently. He handed it to her with the package of socks on top.

"I think I'm going to put on my new socks right now," Theo said. "It's cold outside."

"Yes, it is," the old man said. "Might snow tonight."

Theo sat down on the bench and pulled off her new boots and her old thin socks. She slipped on a new pair of socks and laced up her new boots. When she stood up she couldn't believe how good her feet felt. For three dollars your feet can always feel this good, she told herself. She folded her old socks neatly and tucked them into her old shoes in the box.

"Thanks," she said to the old man, smiling before she left the store.

"Thank you," he said, waving good-bye.

Theo walked back down 4th Avenue toward home. She could tell it was going to snow by the dark sky and the drop in temperature. People rushed by with their faces covered in scarves. Theo passed a shop that said BUTCHER in gold letters on the window. Inside, a bunch of young boys in bloodsmeared aprons and perfect fade haircuts were hunched over, working. She went in; the door jingled as it closed behind her.

Theo pulled a ticket from the red machine to wait her turn, #83. The glass case in front of her was piled high with beautiful red meat. She would buy three steaks. One each for her and Sammy and Cary Grant, and they would celebrate her good fortune at the OTB. While Theo waited she perused the shelves of imported Italian groceries: ladyfingers and anchovies and olives and cauliflower and peppers soaking in brine. She was filled with a manic euphoria—the kind she'd read about in books, what a poet or painter or musician might feel right before some big creative breakthrough.

"Eighty-three," a boy behind the counter yelled, and when Theo looked up he said, "What can I get you, brother?"

Theo put a jar of green olives stuffed with garlic on the counter and ordered three T-bone steaks. He grabbed the steaks and wrapped them neatly in butcher paper.

"Anything else?"

"No thanks," Theo said wondering if he'd figured out she wasn't "brother" yet.

"Happy holidays," he said.

She started the short walk home, the steaks in one hand and her old shoes in the other. The snow had begun. Not like Theo had imagined, soft flakes fluttering across the sky and filling the eyelashes of pedestrians; instead it snowed a stinging hail. Theo was happier than she'd ever been, and she set the box with her old shoes and socks on top of a newspaper stand, hoping that someone who needed them would find them.

seven

It's true that anyone could have pest problems in New York, since all the buildings are built right up against each other, but the woman who'd lived in Theo and Sammy's apartment before them had to have been a special kind of slob. Within a week of moving in their eyes had been trained to search for darting roaches and scurrying mice. They kept no trash in the house whatsoever—if they ate a banana they ran the peel immediately outside, and with the exception of the celebratory steaks, they'd stopped cooking in the house altogether. They ate slices of pizza standing against the chain-link fence at the end of the small driveway and bowls of cereal on the broken concrete in the backyard.

Theo heard mice moving through the apartment constantly. She'd catch them darting over to Cary Grant's bowl and retreating with a piece of kibble the size of their heads. Theo tried to imagine being able to eat something the size of her head, a head-size hamburger or donut. They decided to start feeding Cary Grant her meals outside.

Theo went to the library and perused the books on do-it-yourself pest control. She found one called *Little Critter Hunting*, written by a man who'd worked as a termite inspector in Manhattan for over thirty years. He posed on the cover holding a rubber rat and sporting a proud '70s moustache. Each of his hairy forearms was covered in faded blue tattoos. Under the picture it just said, "Bill."

The book was a treasure trove of terrible facts. Bill explained pest reproduction rates as math equations. For every one roach you see, ten trillion more squirm inside your walls. The shoulders on a mouse collapse like a lawn chair in order to allow them to crawl through hairline cracks. There was a whole chapter devoted to which cracks mice prefer when entering your home, and how these cracks are often undetectable to the human eye.

Bill recommended glue traps as the most humane way to get rid of mice, explaining how regular snap traps can only take off a leg, and then you would have the bigger problem of a three-legged bleeding mouse running around your house. Other snap trap casualties included partially caught mice that gnawed their tail or foot off to get free. If a person used the glue trap, as Bill suggested, then they could "humanely" drown the mouse after it was caught, preventing it from suffering. Theo didn't understand how a person would be able to go on normally with their life after drowning a mouse.

With *Little Critter Hunting* in hand, Theo moved on to the library's pet training section. She wanted to teach Cary Grant some tricks and browsed the shelf until her eye caught a book with a picture of a parrot on a tricycle. The world would be a better place if the sidewalks were filled with birds riding tricycles, Theo thought. She pulled the book off the shelf along with a dog training book and headed to the desk. She was surprised to find the librarian was a stunning woman in her mid-thirties, with a light chocolate complexion and shiny dark hair.

"Hello," Theo said, a little bit in shock at the discovery of the good-looking librarian.

"Can I have your card?" the librarian asked.

"I need to get one."

"Oh, okay," she said, getting a form from a drawer and handing it to Theo with a pen.

Theo bent down to fill out the form and could smell the librarian's hair. Or was it perfume? It reminded her of leather, like when she'd unwrapped her new shoes. Either way, it made her want to bury her face in the librarian's hair.

The librarian smiled slightly at Theo, and Theo forced herself to look directly into her eyes when she handed her the completed form.

"Theo," the librarian said, reading her name off the form and peeling a bar code from a sheet of stickers. She affixed one to a new card.

Theo watched her scan *Little Critter Hunting* and then the dog and bird training books.

"Do you have a parrot?" she asked, looking at the picture of the bird on the tricycle.

"No," Theo said, smiling.

She didn't tell the librarian that she wanted to see if it was possible to train a lovebird to ride a miniature tricycle. If a parrot was fucking cute, imagine an even smaller bird on a smaller tricycle. Instead she stood in awkward silence.

The librarian handed her *Little Critter Hunting*, and Theo held it up and said, "I have mice and roaches."

She meant it as a joke, like those were her pets instead of parrots. But too much time had passed and the beautiful librarian didn't get it. Theo worried that now she seemed like some compulsive self-discloser.

"That book gets checked out a lot in this neighborhood. We are in Sunset Park, after all," the librarian said.

Theo smiled, not knowing exactly what she meant. There was a young girl doing homework at a reading table, and a few homeless people sitting in other nooks reading books surrounded by all their possessions in plastic bags.

"If we can put a man on the moon, surely we can teach a lovebird to ride a tiny tin tricycle," Theo said to the librarian.

"Oh, you have a lovebird?"

"No," Theo said. "But I've always wanted one. If a parrot looks cute riding a tricycle, imagine how cute a lovebird would be."

The librarian smiled and said, "I'd like to meet a lovebird that can ride a tricycle."

"If we can put a man on the moon," Theo repeated.

"Some people don't believe we've actually put a man on the moon."

The librarian had said it in a teasing voice. Was she flirting?

"I love conspiracy theories but I don't know about the moon one," Theo said.

"Conspiracy theorists say the shadows from the astronauts' boots are all going the wrong direction. We have a book *all about it* if you're interested."

"What I never understood is why you'd go all the way to the moon just to hit a golf ball. There's something so disgusting about that."

The librarian laughed. If by some terrible government oversight Theo got sent to the moon as an ambassador representing earthly sirma'amsirs she would do something better than hit a golf ball. Maybe eat a hot dog or scratch a lotto ticket or put the tiny blue lovebird on a tiny blue tricycle inside a tiny astronaut's space-proof bubble and set it pedaling across the cratered rock. She wanted to ask the librarian if she'd been allowed to do one thing on the moon what it would be. But she could feel the small of her back starting to sweat the way it did when she got nervous.

"Do you need a bag for the books?" the librarian asked.

"No, thanks."

"I'm Marisol," she reached her hand out towards Theo.

Theo shook her soft hand and was sure now she could feel energy between them.

"So did you just move here?" Marisol asked.

"From San Francisco."

"Oh."

Theo saw something cross Marisol's face but she wasn't sure exactly what it was.

"So do you know anyone here?"

"Not really," Theo said.

"If you want you can meet me at this party Saturday," Marisol said, writing down the address on a piece of paper. "I can introduce you to some people."

"Is it a librarian party?" Theo asked, taking the paper and pushing it into her pocket.

Marisol smiled.

"It's a paella party. Have you ever eaten paella?"

Theo shook her head.

"Oh, then you have to come by."

"Sounds good."

Theo floated out of the library and headed home, her cheeks hot. She had the ability to change her own life, she just had to keep on the same psychic frequency she'd been on since she won the money at the OTB. Now she had new boots and a date! The only thing left to do was get rid of the mice and roaches. She stopped at the hardware store on the way home and bought three tubes of caulking to fill cracks undetectable to the human eye.

⋮

Sammy had been born and raised in Brooklyn, and every story seemed to be peppered with "this guy I know," or "I know this guy." One of these guys had gotten her a bartending job at a shitty strip bar called The Looney Bin and another guy had gotten Theo a job as a janitor at junk-mail factory in Staten Island. It didn't pay a lot, but it was under the table and Theo didn't want to eat up all the money she'd won on Buttermilk.

They were living well together. Sammy focused on teaching Cary Grant tricks when she wasn't taking her massage classes or working, and Theo took on the brunt of the pest control. The only thing in their refrigerator was Coke and a jar of peanut butter for the bait on the snap traps. Theo didn't buy the glue traps because she just couldn't imagine drowning the mouse once it was caught. Thankfully, the snap traps had been working out. When she left the house each day Theo set four around the kitchen safely away from Cary Grant's reach, and when she returned, without fail, all were full. Theo would sweep the mousetraps into a dustpan and run them to the garbage cans.

When Sammy wasn't working they would watch old movies and explore pizza shops in Brooklyn. At first Theo was surprised Sammy didn't have friends. When she told stories about her life she mentioned a variety of people, but these people were no longer around, and when Theo asked about them she was vague about their disappearance.

Theo was her friend now. Really they felt like family, doing everything together. If Theo wasn't cleaning the junk-
mail factory Sammy begged her to come to The Looney Bin
and hang out at the bar during her shift. It killed Theo to see
everyone drinking when she was trying not to, but Sammy
was adamant about wanting her there. She preyed on Theo's
weaknesses, promising her she could chain-smoke and have
as many plates of wings as she wanted from the all-you-can-
eat buffet. So Theo would come and smoke cigarettes, drink
non-alcoholic beer and try to read *Crime and Punishment.*

The Looney Bin was in a building that opened to the
street through a glass door. To the left another glass door
led into The Looney Bin and straight ahead was a staircase
leading to some studio apartments on the next floor. Joey
the bouncer stood in front checking IDs. He looked like a
bouncer, with his shaved head and giant tattooed arms, and
he dated one of the younger strippers at bar. Once Theo and
Sammy walked Cary Grant there during the day to pick up
some money and Joey was on so much cocaine he wouldn't
stop petting the dog. Theo was afraid Cary Grant was going
to bite him so she took the dog outside to wait.

The Looney Bin was so sad it didn't even have a stripper
pole. There were two rooms, one with the bar and chicken
wing buffet, and the other was where women between the
ages of twenty and fifty danced on a low carpeted stage. The
bar stretched the entire length of the room. It was dark inside, not like a bar ambiance but like the lights were broken.
As a result, men sometimes stumbled into each other accidentally while trying to take their drinks to the next room
where the carpeted stage awaited. There were no tables or
chairs in the room with the stage, just a bathroom where a
man could get a discount blowjob.

The Looney Bin wasn't the kind of strip club where women go with their boyfriends on some kind of date. It was a place for men who had no girlfriends. When Theo came to visit Sammy, Joey would hold the glass door open for her like it was Sunday dinner.

"Come on in," he'd say. "Where's the doggy?"

Theo was glad for the darkness inside because she felt self-conscious about being a sirma'amsir in this very macho setting. Sometimes if the bar was crowded she went into the other room and watched the women. Was it possible some of these women were over fifty? They could be Theo's mother, and that made a lot of sense, because when Theo thought about her mother's mouth she thought of how her lips pursed in the same disgusted way. There were always three women dancing, separate from each other, shaking their asses where a few dollar bills hung from their G-strings like lint. One of them had an expression that looked like she'd just caught her kids smoking pot or was pissed that they *still* hadn't cleaned their rooms. Like she'd bitten her tongue for so long she now had a different mouth.

There were so many acquired postures in life. Theo had learned the posture of depression combined with en-durance, and she moved through the world as if it was some kind of zoo, observing the postures of others. She recognized the posture of poverty—the boys on the corner from her old neighborhood—and the upright posture of lucky people who'd been born into such circumstance that they even walked with entitlement. Animals could take on these different postures too—cats who'd taught themselves to run sideways or flatten their bodies to the ground at the sight of a broom, because they'd been shooed or swiped at so many times.

Most of the The Looney Bin patrons were fresh-faced Latinos in bright white jeans who'd drenched themselves in cologne and gelled their hair back perfectly. They drank Coronas with lime segments pushed deep into the bottleneck, and when they were tipsy enough they wandered into the other half of the bar and watched the women dance for a while. Theo saw all these men as gaping wounds who just wanted some woman to touch their head or rub against them and make them feel like kings for a moment.

⋮

Theo asked Sammy to come with her to the paella party but she had to work that night. So she took the train to the Lower East Side alone, feeling a little bit guilty about leaving Cary Grant. The dog had taken to giving her sad looks whenever she left, climbing up on the bed and letting out a giant sigh. Theo didn't know what to bring to the party, so she picked up a six-dollar bottle of wine from the bodega near the intimidating towers of the apartment complexes on Avenue B.

When she found the address, the entrance to the building was through a large metal gate with an intercom. Theo rang the doorbell and waited to be buzzed in. A small walkway led from the first gate to the lobby door, and when the gate buzzed Theo hurried to make it through the second door before the buzzing ended. Her hand was pushing through the second door when she felt the nagging sense that someone was behind her, and when she turned around someone who looked like a junkie was pointing a knife at her stomach.

"Give me your money or I'm going to stab you," the junkie said.

"Money?" Theo said incredulously.

She was only carrying three dollars and the brown bag with a six-dollar bottle of wine.

Theo heard herself repeat, "Money?"

He stepped closer and touched the point of the knife blade to her stomach.

"Give me your money or I'm going to stab you," he said, making his voice quieter this time.

Unlike the times when Theo had been a helpless observer of other people's emergencies, she was now filled with an adrenaline born of outrage. She couldn't help but feel the junkie was a novice; in fact, she'd never been so sure of anything. She was practically clairvoyant as she used her x-ray vision on his fingers that were pinching the handle of the knife flimsily, like an amateur learning to toss a Frisbee.

"Money?" she said again, this time more angrily. Every thirty-cent roll she'd eaten in Yonkers burned inside her, and she wrapped her fingers around the neck of the wine bottle and began to swing it at his head. You can kill a person by hitting them in the head with a bottle. You can smash their skull. Theo knew this as she felt her arm whirl towards his face.

Did the bottle slip out of the bag? Or did she intentionally miss his head and smash it into the wall behind him just to scare him? The bright fluorescent lobby lights reflected off the white tile walls as the dark red wine ran down. Theo watched the junkie's face freeze after the bottle crashed inches from his ear, and then he scampered away and she heard the gate slam shut. Her hands shook from adrenaline as she moved her toe over a broken piece of glass on the floor, making a scraping sound. The thick smell of red wine rose up around her, and something primordial made her want to lick some off the floor—she knew exactly how it would taste.

She'd had many drinking dreams since she'd quit—sometimes she drank accidentally, other times rebelliously with a giant *Fuck You.* The unnerving thing about all the drinking dreams was how she could taste the alcohol, exactly as it had tasted in real life. Upon waking she'd be filled with remorse that she'd given up her tenuous sobriety—only to have that remorse replaced by a sense of awe that her cells, her DNA and her subconscious had all kept such careful catalogs that they could provide, when needed, the exact flavor of a gin she'd drunk once in the tenth grade.

Theo climbed the five flights of stairs to the apartment number on the slip of paper, adrenaline making her knees wobble. The whole way up she said to herself: *bad math.* She'd given up her six-dollar bottle of wine instead of the three dollars in her pocket.

Finally, she reached the landing of the apartment; on the other side of a thick steel door she could hear music and the lively sounds of a party. She rang the doorbell. Someone opened the door and Theo looked in at the room full of strangers. Marisol was kneeling on the floor by an oven, looking inside the broiler to check on a giant pan of paella. The kitchen was full of laughing and chain-smoking dykes, all drinking wine and oblivious to the fact that just moments before there had been a knife pointed at Theo's gut.

"Wow," Marisol said when she looked up and saw Theo in the doorway. "I wasn't sure you would come."

"Hi," Theo responded, suddenly shy.

"This is Theo, everyone," Marisol said.

Theo waved.

"How are you?" Marisol asked.

Theo didn't want to ruin the party but it seemed insane to not share what had just happened to her.

"Um, I just got held up at knifepoint by a junkie in the lobby."

"What?!" everyone screamed.

"I swung a bottle of wine at his head and then he ran out."

"Do you think he's still there?" Marisol asked, and then some dykes bolted downstairs.

The girl who had opened the door gave up her chair and sat Theo down.

"Let me make you a drink. What are you drinking?" she asked.

Theo was trying to light a match but her hands were shaking too much. She didn't want to cry, and she felt the adrenaline moving her in that direction.

Marisol took the cigarette from her and lit it, handing it back with a shot of tequila.

The smell of tequila rose to Theo's nose. She hated tequila. On her sixteenth birthday she'd drunk so much of it that she passed out facedown on the beach, alcohol poisoned. The police had plucked up her body and rushed her to the hospital.

"I think I just want a Coke right now," she told Marisol, avoiding the conversation about the tequila.

The dykes came back from the lobby, reporting what Theo already knew to be true, that the junkie was long gone and the only thing that remained was the bright tile wall streaked with red wine and the brown paper bag and shattered glass lying in a puddle on the floor. Theo recounted the story to the roomful of strangers, downing her can of Coke and chain-smoking as they listened. Then she explained to the horrified group how she'd found herself renting a room in Yonkers that had carpet the color of Ronald McDonald's hair and working for a boss who called people *You Fucking*

Faggot all day and how Theo had confronted him in her calmest voice, telling him she was gay and his use of the word *faggot* upset her. When she'd finished, he'd nodded his head contritely and apologized. Then he opened his desk drawer, pulled out a *Playboy* magazine and tossed it at her, saying, "I bet you would like some of the toys in here!"

"You could sue him," Marisol said.

Theo would never have read Marisol as queer if she hadn't flirted with her. And she was stunned at how nice the strangers at the party were. They all seemed interested in offering her solutions to improve her life and giving her drinks. At various points throughout the evening someone else handed Theo a freshly poured glass of wine and Theo, who'd become tired of saying, "I'm not drinking," instead said, "Thank you," promptly abandoning the glass among a sea of others where someone would eventually mistake it for their own.

When the party was over Marisol asked Theo if she was heading back to Brooklyn. They walked to the subway together shyly, Theo reviewing the wide array of emotions the night had held. Her lungs hurt from smoking. She wanted to hold Marisol's hand but the train was packed with people drunk from holiday parties. She'd caught one of the guys checking out Marisol, and now she felt self-conscious.

As they pulled into the 53rd Street station, Theo stood up.

"Will you give me your phone number?" she asked Marisol.

"You're not going to ask me to come home with you?"

"I am," Theo said. "But just not tonight."

Marisol took a pen out of her purse and wrote her phone number on a cigarette, handing it to Theo.

Theo stood on the platform holding Marisol's gaze

through the window until the train had pulled out of the station. On the walk home she was a mix of excitement about Marisol and fear that behind every shadow was a man with a knife. She hurried home to a sleeping Cary Grant. She petted the dog's side until Cary Grant woke up, beating her tail wildly into the bed.

"Hello, good dog," Theo said quietly.

She let the dog into the backyard and stood in the cold while she went to the bathroom. There was no way she was going to walk Cary Grant down the street at 2 AM. When she walked back in the house she could see the mousetraps were all full but she didn't have the energy to empty them. Cary Grant hopped back into bed waiting for her. She had taken to pawing at Theo or Sammy when she wanted them to lift up the comforter so she could go underneath. Theo let her under and the dog curled in a circle and plastered her body against hers.

"Someone pulled a knife on me," Theo whispered stroking Cary Grant's ribs.

While she stared at the ceiling waiting for Sammy to come home she wondered if anyone had cleaned up the broken wine bottle in the lobby.

eight

Theo looked at Marisol's phone number all day but could not muster the courage to call her. What if she called and Marisol had lost interest? Then her good luck streak would be over. She told Sammy she was going to take her out to dinner to celebrate getting her first A on a Reiki test. She was happy for Sammy, but it filled her with panic when it seemed like other people had embarked on a plan for life while she had none. When Sammy said, "I love massage school," Theo heard, "Theo, you don't have a plan for life."

The closest Theo had come to a dream was to be an artist, but she had no talent. She tried to learn to draw, practicing collages or charcoal outlines of Styrofoam cones alone and in classes at the community college. *Anyone can learn to draw. Learning to draw is just learning to see.* That's what every teacher said. But for Theo it wasn't true. No matter how hard she tried, she was unable to transfer the pictures she saw in her head onto paper, and her teachers didn't encourage her.

Still, Henry Darger and Vincent Van Gogh were her heroes. Darger had been a janitor for sixty-seven years, and Van Gogh unable to earn money in his lifetime, or to do anything else than just paint and live with coal miners and see prostitutes and lick turpentine from his brushes. In the end, Darger would've been just a creepy janitor, and Van Gogh, a redhead who enjoyed a prostitute, if no one had canonized their work. Theo loved the swirling brushstrokes of Van Gogh's skies, bedposts and floorboards. She wanted to eat the canvases, they were so thick with paint. She wanted to live in his bedrooms, sleep in his four-poster beds, wear his little black boots. But Darger and Van Gogh were famous men, and Theo, a timid sirma'amsir who had spent her life at jobs in party stores, parking lots, hospital cafeterias, night hotel desks, and any other place that would afford her time alone to read about these men she could never be.

Theo swept up four dead mice and reset the traps, and she and Sammy headed out to Bay Ridge where a restaurant was having a lobster night. A banner hung outside announcing, *Monday Night! One-pound lobsters for $5.99!* Theo and Sammy entered through giant French doors. Votive candles flickered on all the tables. They sat down at a small table by the wall, and Sammy looked at the extensive tap beer menu.

A waiter came over to take their drink order, and it took Theo a moment to recognize him.

"Big Vic!" she said. "Do you remember me?"

"What's up?" he smiled, shaking her hand.

"This is the guy who I met at the OTB," Theo told Sammy.

"Victor," Big Vic said, extending his hand to Sammy.

"Sammy."

"I'm actually going to Atlantic City tonight," Big Vic said.

"Really?" Theo asked.

"After work. I'm gonna take the bus," Big Vic said. "You guys should come."

"Maybe," Theo heard herself say. "We'll think about it."

"We were going to get the lobster special," Sammy said.

Theo could tell Sammy was having a low-blood-sugar moment. Big Vic looked over his shoulder nervously at a man sitting at the end of the bar and then said, "Don't do that."

"How come?" Theo asked.

"Well," he looked afraid, "the owner is kind of a scumbag and he buys half the lobsters dead. A guy just sent his back because the inside looked like mashed potatoes."

"No," Sammy said laughing.

Big Vic smiled and nodded.

"And sometimes there's this weird green stuff inside. And when I told the owner he was just like, 'Tell them that's what the females look like. That they're pregnant and those are the eggs.'"

Sammy was laughing harder now. "Those are the females," she intoned in her best nature documentary voice.

Big Vic smiled, flashing the gap in his teeth.

"She's stoned," Theo said, explaining Sammy's giggling. "So what should we eat?"

"I'll hook you up," Big Vic said taking their menus.

He returned a short while later with a pitcher of stout, two glasses, a plate of nachos, wings, and BBQ pork sandwiches.

Theo watched Sammy pour the dark beer into her glass and take a big gulp.

"You want a Coke, girl?" Sammy asked

"I'm not sure," Theo said, fixating on the pitcher of beer. She could conjure the exact bitter taste of it.

What had seemed so clear when she left San Francisco—she must not drink alcohol ever again, no matter what—now felt like incomprehensible dream logic. Plus, she had never exactly told Sammy she was trying to be on the wagon or that she'd quit drinking many times before. Theo reached across the table and grabbed the pitcher, pouring herself a glass.

"Just because you poured it doesn't mean you have to drink it," she told herself.

But she'd already taken the drink when she ran toward the first thought instead of away. Now it was just a formality to swallow the beer.

"I thought you didn't like beer," Sammy said.

The worst thing that can happen to someone who quits drinking and then decides to drink again is when people start questioning that decision as a glass is raised. Theo ignored Sammy and took a big swallow of her beer. She waited to feel regret or happiness or relief—all emotions she'd felt before when she'd decided to say fuck it and crash a bottle over herself like she was a yacht, but this time she strangely felt nothing except the bitter beer dripping down the back of her throat.

"Maybe I'm not an alcoholic anymore," she thought, and the whole world cracked wide open. *People are alcoholics if they let themselves be alcoholics. Americans are so busy pathologizing everything.* Theo let the warm blanket of beer drape over her brain.

By the time dinner was over Sammy was sleepy and no longer wanted to take an impromptu trip to Atlantic City. Theo drove her home, got her envelope of cash, and emptied the mousetraps. When she went to sweep up the last one she saw that the mouse was still alive.

"Girl!" she screamed, and Sammy hung back in the doorway timidly.

"Girl, what?"

"It only caught half the body!"

The mouse lay very still until Theo tried to get close and then it squirmed and flashed its tiny beady eye at her in fear. She started crying.

"What should I do, girl?" Theo asked.

"I don't know girl."

"Get me a bag. You have to help me. I need your help."

Theo didn't feel drunk from the beer, just a familiar heavy despondency in her body.

Sammy returned with a plastic bag.

"You have to hold it open. I'm going to sweep the mouse into the dustpan and then put it in the bag, okay? All you have to do is hold the bag open and then I'll take care of the rest."

"Girl," Sammy said, stuck on repeat.

Theo moved the broom around the back of the stove and swept the mouse out while Cary Grant watched. She didn't want the dog to see the mouse squirm and then have this whole situation go from bad to worse if she had some kind of prey instinct.

"I'm so sorry," Theo told the mouse, dumping the whole trap into the plastic bag.

She set down the dustpan and took the bag from Sammy, who was standing pale and frozen. Outside, she dropped it into the trash can. If only she'd listened to Bill about the glue traps. She knew she should do something now to put the mouse out of its misery, drop a rock, or get a hammer, but she couldn't, so she went back into the house sobbing. She couldn't believe she'd let herself start drinking again. When she came back inside Sammy was standing behind the bar making herself a drink with a martini shaker she'd bought at IKEA.

"Want a drink, girl?" she said.

Theo nodded. "Make mine out of gin," she said.

⋮

Theo sat at the bar drinking her martini and staring at Marisol's phone number written on the cigarette.

"Should I call her?" she asked Sammy.

"You better hurry. It's almost ten and she's a librarian, right?"

"Should I ask her to go to Atlantic City?"

"No," Sammy said. "With Big Vic? Maybe that's not a good first date."

Theo nodded and put the cigarette inside the envelope of cash in her jacket pocket. She had about $3,500 left from her Buttermilk winnings. Even though she didn't want to separate the lucky bills she counted out a thousand dollars and put it in her coffee can in case she came into some bad luck.

"Will you let Cary Grant sleep under the covers?" she asked Sammy.

"Of course. Have fun, girl."

Theo picked Big Vic up from work when he got off—driving would be faster than taking the bus. On the drive he told her about himself: He was twenty-three and had lived with his girlfriend in an apartment with no heat since he was eighteen; every night she makes him dinner even though he gets a free meal from work. He eats after his shift and then goes home and eats again, because he doesn't want to let her down. He'd lied about where he was going tonight, telling her he was spending the night at his mom's; his mother was confined to a wheelchair from a premature stroke. In fact, tomorrow he was supposed to meet a guy so he could buy a minivan for when he takes her to her doctor's appointments in the wheelchair. He already bought his girlfriend a leather jacket for Christmas: "It's nice. It's not for standing on the corner."

Big Vic had played baseball his whole life; he was a pretty decent third base. A few years back some scouts from the Atlanta Braves farm team had looked at him. But when Theo tried to get him to talk about it more, he wouldn't. It was a two-and-a-half-hour drive to Atlantic City, and after the first fifteen minutes they didn't say much more to each other except when Big Vic asked if Sammy was her girl.

"No, she's like my brother. We met in jail."

Big Vic's eyes got big and Theo said, "It's not as dramatic as it sounds. I like a different girl." She wished Marisol were in the truck with them.

"It's so weird we're going to Atlantic City together," she said. "We don't even know each other."

"You're lucky, girl. We're a team. We're gonna win that money tonight!"

"Cha-Ching!" Theo said, and they high-fived.

By the time they could see the lights of Atlantic City they'd both gotten their second wind. Big Vic went straight to the blackjack table while Theo sat down at a Wheel of Fortune slot machine. The casino was decorated for Christmas and full of people sitting alone.

Theo heard a cocktail waitress say, "Cocktails, cocktails," as if she were a bird mother calling to Theo, her lost bird child who'd fluttered into low foliage to hide her broken wings.

"Cocktails?" the waitress said looking right into Theo's eyes. She was wearing a red Santa hat that said NAUGHTY.

"Gin and tonic, please."

I can quit drinking again tomorrow, she thought, lighting a cigarette and feeding one of the new hundred-dollar bills she'd won at the OTB into her Wheel of Fortune slot machine. Lucky money. Lucky money, Theo thought. The machine registered 400 credits and then shouted, *WHEEL. OF. FORTUNE!* so loudly Theo jumped back. Had she won something already? She was confused and looked at a woman at the end of her row who was scowling into the screen of her own slot machine and slamming her hand down on the play buttons, making a slap sound each time she did so.

"Well, Merry Christmas," Theo thought, looking away quickly from the woman's bad vibes.

Theo pushed the SPIN button and watched the three wheels whirl to a halt. Nothing, so she hit the button again. A red seven, a blue seven and an orange. It seemed like something, but the red block numbers that kept track of her credits only dwindled. She read the game rules printed on the side of the slot machine. In order to win, she needed the special Wheel of Fortune symbol to stop exactly in the middle of the black line on the third wheel. Then she would enter the bonus round and hit the SPIN button again and it would activate the giant wheel on top of her slot machine. Her grumpy neighbor had just activated the bonus round and her machine had shouted, *WHEEL. OF. FORTUNE!* The woman did an elaborate superstitious hand movement, wiggling her fingertips at the screen before pressing the SPIN button. The simulated sound of a wheel ticking very fast started up, and as the ticking slowed, so did the wheel, waiting to settle on the winning amount. A person could win from 25 to 10,000 quarters. And of course the 10,000 was placed in a slot between 25 and 30.

"C'mon, Wheel!" Theo heard herself squeal, rooting for the woman. She felt her blood rise as she saw the woman's wheel settling near 10,000 quarters.

"Stop, stop, stop!" the woman screamed futilely as the wheel settled on 30. She'd won 30 quarters.

"Goddamn you!" she screamed at the machine.

Theo wanted to say: *It could be worse, you could've won 25 quarters.*

Then the woman reached into her purse and fed a crisp hundred-dollar bill into the machine, even though she still had credits left.

Theo wanted to move to get away from the woman's bad vibes. Plus, she wondered if Big Vic was winning. With the exception of winning four quarters on a single cherry, she'd gotten nothing from her machine. The colorful Wheel of Fortune symbol that reminded Theo of some kind of tool for teaching people to learn fractions kept landing just above and just below the black line. The first time it happened her heart leapt and she had paused, waiting for a chance to enter the bonus round. But now she understood the machine was trying to trick her, letting the symbol appear like a carrot before a horse. Even though she wanted to leave the machine she was afraid to, because what if it suddenly hit? She'd already invested some money in it.

The Sexy Santa cocktail waitress came back with Theo's gin and tonic, and Theo realized she didn't have any singles to tip her.

"Hang on a second," she said, standing up. She pulled a hundred-dollar bill from the envelope in her coat and handed it to the waitress, "Merry Christmas."

The waitress looked at her a second, said, "Thanks," and walked off with a tray full of drinks.

Theo felt pissed. The waitress could've been more grateful. Maybe she thought Theo was pathetic and trying to hit on her or she hated gay people. She cashed out her machine and decided to follow the waitress, who had a couple of non-alcoholic beers on her tray. She'd drunk them too when she first got sober, and remembered someone telling her, "non-alcoholic beer is for non-alcoholics." She didn't quite understand what that meant, but back when she was trying to stay out of the bars, she'd sit home and drink a six-pack of non-alcoholic beer each night. She didn't need an addiction specialist to tell her there was something fucked up about that. The cocktail waitress disappeared into a VIP blackjack area.

Theo downed her gin and tonic as she walked and searched the blackjack tables for Big Vic. When she couldn't find him she sat down at a dollar slot machine and removed another hundred-dollar bill from her envelope. The first time Theo saw someone feed a hundred-dollar bill into a slot machine she'd thought she would die. It was like the first time she saw someone step over a sleeping homeless person while holding a Frappuccino and giggling indifferently with a friend, or the first time she learned that a senior citizen would sign over their entire monthly Social Security check to a bar and draw upon it as the month went by, or the first time she found out people got paid fifty dollars an hour to do nothing in offices while the rest of the world scrubbed toilets for pennies. At that point Theo had never put a hundred-dollar bill into a slot machine, but she'd put five twenty-dollar bills in such quick succession she might as well have. And when she realized that, she thought *why split hairs.*

The next slot machine was old-fashioned, with lucky sevens and a variety of fruit. Theo pulled the handle again and again, trying to get three sevens. She was numb, winning nothing, her tongue thick with gin and tonic. The red numbers that displayed her credits were dwindling. She pulled and she pulled and she pulled, and each time she pulled it cost her three dollars. When she'd depleted her credits down to two, she pulled the handle one more time, and when she did she prayed, "Please, please, please God, I'll quit drinking again tomorrow if you let me win this right now," and just then three red sevens fell into perfect place. Her heart leapt and she grabbed the elbow of the woman sitting next to her, out of impulse, like one might grab the arm of a seatmate on a bumpy airplane flight, and she waited to hear the mad dinging of a victory, but nothing happened.

The woman looked at Theo's machine while still playing her own and said, "Why did you do that? Why weren't you playing the maximum amount of credits?"

"What do you mean?"

"You have to play three credits to win on three sevens. Otherwise you get nothing."

"It was my last two credits," Theo defended.

"You don't win anything when you're only playing two credits. You can't do that. You'll kill yourself doing that," the woman said. "That's the kind of stuff that keeps you up at night."

Theo stared at the three sevens, stunned, and kept pushing the SPIN button even though there was no money left. When she finally got up to leave, the woman told her one more time, "You can't do that," shaking her head.

Theo wandered over to the pay phones and stood in front of one for a long time holding the cigarette with Marisol's phone number. She'd just call her and say hi even though it was late. She had no idea what time it was, but she knew it had to be at least 2 AM. She dialed the number and hung up when she realized she didn't have any change. She considered breaking another hundred and getting some rolls of quarters from the change girl, but felt impatient. She dialed the operator and asked to place a collect call. While the operator dialed Theo's heart pounded. She wanted to hear Marisol's voice. She regretted having come to Atlantic City.

Marisol's sleepy voice answered.

"Will you accept a collect call from Theo?" the operator said.

Marisol paused a second and gave out a little chuckle, "Uh, okay."

"You are connected," the operator said, hanging up.

"Hi," Theo said.

"Hello."

"What are you doing?"

"I'm sleeping. What are you doing?"

"I'm in Atlantic City."

"Really?"

Theo couldn't tell if there was the slight sound of disgust in her voice.

"I just wanted to call because I wanted to call you all day and, uh, I didn't."

"That's nice."

"So, maybe we can do something again soon?"

"Yeah," Marisol said, "why don't you call me when you're back from Atlantic City."

"Okay. And I'll give you money for this collect call. I just didn't have any change."

"Sounds good. I'm going to go back to sleep now because I have to work in the morning."

"Okay. Goodnight."

"Goodnight."

Theo felt injured walking away from the pay phones. She didn't know what she had expected, but that wasn't it. She wandered through the casino slightly depressed until she found Big Vic at a blackjack table looking pissed. She stood back watching him bust a few hands, throwing his cards down in disgust and occasionally taking a sip of a Coke. She couldn't understand how he could refuse free drinks from a casino that was so obviously kicking his ass. Theo had never been too proud to refuse a free four-hundred-dollar gin and tonic. While she stood behind him, his losing streak continued. Bust. Bust. Bust. Even the dealer was disgusted. Nobody tips the dealer when they're losing. Theo watched the dealer's face and saw that she was afraid to turn over her own cards because she couldn't stop winning. After Big Vic was out of chips he opened his wallet to buy more, but the only thing inside was a condom. Then he reached into his pockets and rummaged around, confirming the fact that he was a broke-ass joke.

"Let's go," he said to Theo, and they left the casino.

On the walk to the truck Big Vic confessed he'd lost eighteen hundred dollars. She didn't say anything because she knew there's nothing to say to a person who's lost that much.

"That was the money I was going to use to buy my mom a minivan tomorrow," he said in the very, very, very low voice of someone who has lost a lot of money.

"You have to work tomorrow?" Theo asked.

He shook his head no.

"Let's get a room, take a shower. Maybe eat something. I'll loan you two hundred dollars and we'll win that money back. It's lucky money," Theo said, patting her jacket pocket where the envelope of Buttermilk winnings remained.

"No," Big Vic said, but she could see he was considering it.

⋮

Theo realized it was 4 AM and they would have to check out of a room by noon, so they decided to try plan B, which was get some pizza and use the money they would have spent on a room to recoup their losses at the roulette wheel. Big Vic sat in angry silence next to Theo on the ride to the pizza shop. It was the last bit of night where it meets up with morning, the sun about to push up against black sky. Theo felt crazy from exhaustion and cigarettes and alcohol and the casino. But the biggest disappointment was her conversation with Marisol.

What had she wanted, for Marisol to beg her to come over right then and marry her? She thought about it for a second and, embarrassed, acknowledged yes. Maybe she should have sex with Big Vic and that would make her less attached to Marisol. She'd had sex with a few guys in high school, but mostly during alcoholic blackouts. Now that she was drinking again anything could be normal. She had become a ghost walking beside her ghost self; when you're a ghost you can be anything. She could be in love with Big Vic and help him care for his mother. She could be a professional gambler or a day trader. Someone could surely teach her how to be a day trader. Plus, maybe Big Vic just needed sex to quell his post-gambling rage. She had no idea how men operated, she just figured they were willing to have sex anytime anywhere, especially after she'd seen the inexplicable desires of men at The Looney Bin.

The farther away from the casino they got, the more real became the fact that Big Vic had lost the eighteen hundred dollars he was going to use to buy his mother a van. Theo knew from her own experience of losing large sums of money that there were no words to console him. It would take him a long time schlepping dead lobsters at the restaurant to recoup those losses. But money stops being money in casinos and becomes this weird other currency of easy come/easy go credits.

The first time Theo lost eighteen hundred dollars she felt like she would kill herself. Tonight, the combination of losing four hundred dollars plus her shitty phone call with Marisol and her botched sobriety made her only *consider* suicide, eyeing the ditches on the side of the road. She absorbed Big Vic's despair, and the trees flew past the windows. She wondered if everyone in the long line of cars heading away from the casino at 4 AM was considering the same thing. Finally, they reached the 24-hour pizza place.

Theo gave Big Vic a hundred-dollar bill and asked him to go in while she stood against her truck smoking her ten millionth cigarette of the night. He emerged holding two white paper bags, and half tossed/half flung Theo's on the hood of the truck. Inside was a giant, greasy slice of pizza.

"If he asks me, I'll have sex with him," she thought, interpreting the toss of the pizza as some kind of mating call.

They ate their pizza and downed some soda and then Theo turned to Big Vic and said, "Scared money don't win."

⋮

Every casino smells the same: cigarette smoke and carpet glue and doom. Theo knew it was a lie when Big Vic said he was trying to win money to help support his mother or girlfriend. She also knew she was lying when she said the reason she was returning to the casino was to help Big Vic. Gambling is not about getting money; it's about shoving adrenaline into the brain receptor that eats it up like birthday cake.

"We're going right to the roulette wheel," Theo said. "That's the only way to do this."

Because it was so early in the morning there was only one roulette wheel in operation. An older Asian man sat on a stool and chain-smoked next to a tray with an untouched steak dinner on it. Theo took a hundred-dollar bill out of her envelope and bought four twenty-five dollar chips, placing them all on black.

"Oh man," Big Vic said.

"Scared money don't win," Theo said, looking him in the eye.

"Okay, okay. Come on baby," Big Vic said.

If they still had money then they still had hope. The croupier spun the wheel and they all watched the silver ball bounce around inside it.

"Black, black, black," Theo whispered, trying to will the ball to settle into the black slot.

"Black twenty-eight," the croupier sang.

"Yes!" Big Vic cried.

The croupier slid two matching towers of chips over to Theo's pile and then spun the wheel again.

"You gonna let all that ride?" Big Vic asked.

Theo didn't answer him, just watched the wheel turn and in her mind repeated, *black, black, black*.

"Black fifteen."

"Oh shit," Big Vic said.

The Asian man got a big payout because he had a lot of money on fifteen. Theo and Big Vic watched the croupier measure stacks and push them over to him. Theo's low back was sweating. She left the chips where they were, and the croupier spun the wheel again, and as it slowed Theo could see the ball settling in the red seven. *Black, black, black,* she thought, closing her eyes.

"Black eleven," the croupier called out.

Big Vic slapped Theo's shoulder.

Theo resisted breaking the streak but she really wanted to put a hundred-dollar chip on eight. The croupier spun the wheel again and she watched the ball bounce around, and then right before it was too late to place anymore bets, she put a hundred-dollar chip on the number eight. She watched the ball bounce around. She was so high, endorphins were racing through her brain like a bunch of elementary school kids during recess.

"Black eight!"

"Fucking shit! That's thirty-five hundred dollars," Theo said to Big Vic, "just for the eight!"

Big Vic was so high that he turned around in a small circle of disbelief, flashing the gap in his teeth.

"Cash out," he told Theo. "Cash out."

"Are you kidding? Let's do one more."

"No. We gotta get out of here before we lose it."

The Asian man used the delay in action to saw off a piece of his cold, untouched steak and numbly chew it. When a cocktail waitress came by, he signaled for her to take it away.

"Cash out," Theo told the croupier.

Her body buzzed with adrenaline as she watched the croupier push a tower of black chips toward her. She pulled two hundred-dollar chips off the top, tapped them twice on the felt and rolled them to the side for him.

"Thank you," the croupier said.

Then she picked up the rest of her chips and stepped back from the table.

"How much is there?" Big Vic asked.

"I don't know. I just want to watch and see if black comes up again."

She could see the relief in his face and they waited to see where the ball would fall next. The Asian man glanced at Theo and then put a hundred-dollar chip on her eight that just won.

"That eight better not hit again," Theo said to Big Vic.

The croupier spun the wheel and they all watched the silver ball bounce around.

"Black twenty-eight," the croupier sang.

He was like an experimental poet reciting to an audience of one.

"It's still coming up black. We should've let all that ride," Theo said sadly.

"No, no. We're straight," Big Vic said, giving Theo a celebratory jab in the arm.

She counted out eighteen hundred-dollar chips and held onto the rest as they went to cash them out at the window. After paying Big Vic, she had won $3,100. While she waited for the cashier to pay her she was trying to calculate how much she would have won if she'd let the money ride one more time.

On the drive back to Brooklyn, Theo tried to make Big Vic talk to her so she wouldn't fall asleep, but before long he'd passed out with his head pressed into the window. The rest of the ride she obsessed about Marisol. She would take her out to a fancy dinner with her winnings. It was morning rush hour when they reached the city. Everyone in the cars around them had the sleepy faces of people heading to work. Big Vic asked Theo if she could drop him at a subway station. He was getting dental work done at the Bellevue dental clinic. Then he was going to buy a minivan for his mom.

nine

Theo slept late into the afternoon, waking up confused. She felt hungover, something she hadn't experienced in a long time. Slowly she began playing back the events of the night before, squashing out the bad feelings about drunk-dialing Marisol by focusing on the fact that she'd won another $3,100. She got into the shower and tried to scrub off the smoke from the casino. She would bring Marisol flowers and return her books to the library. But first she needed a haircut.

Theo had always picked her barbers the same way she picked her therapists: less than fifteen dollars and a vacant chair. Because of this she often met sad barbers who drank coffee out of dirty cups and read magazines that had hit the stands thirty years ago. Barbershops were dangerous watering holes, where predators waited in hiding for the timid sirma'amsir to come and drink. She came from a long line of barbers and hairstylists—in fact, she'd considered becoming a barber herself. She'd gone to man barbers and woman barbers, friend barbers and stranger barbers who asked was she on her lunch break, did she speak Spanish, have any children, go to church, know how to drive, have rent control?

She gave vague instructions, "Number two on the sides

and natural in the back." If asked straight sideburn or angle sideburn, she'd say straight. If asked square back or natural back, she'd say natural. She'd had her hair cut by religious women whose shop walls were so completely covered with Psalms posters, there was barely room for all the crucifixes. She'd had her hair cut in kitchens, in discount haircutting franchises by Russian students, by women who looked at her and told her to bleach her hair, or at the very least try a few highlights, and they said it without malice, as one woman to another. They told her because they'd bleached their own hair, to get a man or keep a man, and Theo knew that when they looked at her she seemed like some kind of terrifying exotic food dish, like pig nipple, or brain, or eyeball or tenderloin of sirma'amsir served with mint jelly, and they combed her thick fur this way and that and hung their heads over her shoulder asking if she was absolutely sure she didn't want highlights, and they said it with an open heart: They wanted Theo to be able to seize a man, any man, because they were absolutely positive there was no way a person who looked like Theo had a man. Or maybe they wanted Theo to be a woman, and when they looked at her they had no fucking idea how to begin making that happen, so they thought they could chip away at it by starting with highlights. And for the most part Theo couldn't hate those women, because she could see the goodwill in their eyes.

Sometimes she would go to Mary's, where the men's haircuts were ten and the women's twelve, and when she got to the register to pay there would be a giant debate of *diez o doce, diez o doce?* And ultimately it was *doce*, the timid sirma'amsir too timid to object to a two-dollar surcharge.

Today Theo wanted a haircut so she could feel handsome enough when she asked Marisol out. She walked up to 4th Avenue and found a shop where the barber had just finished giving a buzz cut to a redheaded man. Theo looked at a few handmade signs posted on the mirrors that said the prices of haircuts had just gone up from eight to ten dollars. The shop thanked the customers in advance for their loyalty. The man who'd left his tufts of red hair on the ground didn't have enough money for a tip because he hadn't known about the price change. He looked sheepish, gave the short, old, sad barber the money he had, saying, "I'll come back after I eat lunch," which Theo doubted.

The barber motioned Theo into the chair, and as always when she climbed into these chairs, she slumped forward with a submissive posture, curling her body into its most unobtrusive shape, not knowing if the barber thought of her as a man or a woman.

"What you want?" the barber asked.

She tried to figure out the man's ethnicity but could not. She guessed Filipino.

"Number two," she said.

"And nothing off the top," the barber said, more as a command then a question.

"Right," Theo said, even though she did need the top trimmed.

The barber started to buzz the sides of her hair with the number two attachment. She watched him slyly in the mirror then glanced through the front window to the street. There was a perfect spiderweb shatter from a bullet that had been halfheartedly covered with a calendar. The barber was using only one of his hands to do everything, and she wondered if he was paralyzed. In San Francisco there had been a paralyzed barber. Her friends went to him but she'd never been because he was a few blocks farther than she'd wanted to walk. He'd had a stroke but kept on working, modifying, holding things with his shoulder to his bent neck and one good hand.

Paralyzed barber or not, Theo was happy with this haircut. She could tell from how the hair was falling off easily that the man had good buzzers. She caught a glimpse of the dark circles under her eyes, a result of her all-nighter in Atlantic City. Barbershop mirrors were especially abusive to the timid sirma'amsir, how they showed every flaw.

There was a haircut called *The Butch* on the poster on the wall. *The Butch* was next to *The Flat Top* and *The Brush Cut*. Honestly, she couldn't tell the difference between any of them. Nor did she think the man in the illustration of *Haircuts For Large Ears* seemed to have large ears at all. Theo looked at her ears and wondered if they would be considered large. It amazed her how many times she'd seen this exact same yellowed poster advertising *Haircuts For Large Ears, Haircuts For Small Ears, The Flat Top, The Professional,* and *The JFK*. This neighborhood was Puerto Rican and Dominican; still, the poster on the wall offered choices for white men with blond hair from fifty years ago. If a person didn't want a haircut from the 1950s, they could choose from some photographs that were taped to the mirror of clients who'd gotten sports team logos shaved into their heads.

Theo was looking at the shots of young men who'd gotten New York Yankees symbols buzzed into their heads when she heard the buzzer stop and the shop door open.

A man on crutches came in, pulled a blue bottle out of the side pocket of his backpack and said, "Can I leave this here?"

He seemed sketchy. The barber looked at him as if he were a fly circling his dinner, not quite close enough to swat.

"I'm gonna leave this here, okay?" the man said again holding out the blue bottle.

The barber glanced at him, turned his buzzer back on and continued to circle around Theo's head with his one arm. The man crutched forward and now Theo knew he was on something because he had a relaxed, underwater opiated speech that Theo recognized. She wondered why a man who was carrying an entire backpack would feel as if that bottle was the one thing weighing him down. Maybe there was something hidden inside it, like drugs. He took another crutch step into the shop, and Theo watched the barber continue to ignore him as he set his water bottle down on the windowsill.

The barber flicked his eyes at the man, and the man mumbled, "This is dangerous," and lifted the crutch straight out, pointing the tip at the barber like a child pretending he has a gun.

The barber finished with the buzzers and fumbled around in his drawer.

Theo took the barber's cue and feigned indifference. She realized the man wasn't threatening them—he was showing them that the metal had pushed through the rubber stopper at the bottom and he didn't want to walk on the tile floor with his broken crutch.

"I'll come back tomorrow for that," he said, pulling the barbershop door closed. The barber watched him go, continuing his fumbling in the drawer. With great effort he lifted an enormous pair of scissors. They seemed like a joke, something to trim a hedge. Now Theo could see there was something physically wrong with his hand—the effort it took, how he steadied the scissors with his other hand like a paw. For a second she worried about getting a haircut from a man who didn't have two functioning hands, but of all the places Theo stuffed her feelings, barbershops were at the top of the list.

She wanted to make small talk with the barber, ask him if he'd ever seen the movie *Giant*. Theo and Sammy had gone to see it earlier in the week at the movie house that showed old movies, and two-thirds of the way through the screen had turned into psychedelic garble and the house manager had come out to say the reel had been chewed up in the projector. Everyone got coupons for free popcorn and a movie. She and Sammy couldn't believe they weren't going to see how the movie ended.

"Have you been busy because of the holidays?" Theo started.

The barber turned off the buzzer and looked at Theo.

"Off the top?" he said.

"Yes," Theo said, watching him touch his ear. She realized he was wearing a hearing aid.

"This much," he said, holding a few inches between his fingertips.

"Okay," Theo said.

He nodded and picked up the hedge trimmers again. Theo watched him hack at her hair like it was some sort of irritating weed in his vegetable garden and was thankful when he put the hedge trimmers down. She studied her haircut in the mirror and was surprised how good it looked considering her fears. The barber unbuttoned her drape and began to lather her neck and face with shaving cream. Never in her life as a sirma'amsir had someone tried to shave her face. *He thinks I'm a man* Theo thought as she watched him open the straight razor. He steadied the open blade in his good hand with his bad hand.

"Everything's fine," she thought, her heart pounding.

"If it's my fate to have my throat slit open by a paralyzed barber while getting my face shaved, so be it."

The barber pulled the straight razor down the side of her face under her sideburns, and she sat there listening to the sound of the blade scraping her skin. Then he dragged it down the other side, continuing until all of the shaving cream was gone. He took a bottle of bright blue tonic and dribbled some on his hand and slapped the sides of Theo's face until the skin tingled. Then he put his fingers on her head and rubbed her scalp. When he was all finished Theo said, "Thank you."

The barber touched his hearing aid again, and said, "Ten dollars."

She pulled a hundred-dollar bill from her pocket and handed it to him.

He made a face and then turned to his cash box to root around for change.

"Keep the change. Merry Christmas," she said.

Theo walked out, her face still tingling with the tonic.

⋮

It felt good to give her winnings away. Plus, she had so many hundred-dollar bills there seemed no end to them. Theo left the barbershop feeling dapper and grateful to be alive, but when she got within a few blocks of the library she felt her stomach starting to get nervous. She stopped at a display of flowers outside a bodega, settling on a bunch of variegated yellow-and-orange roses. She paid for them and battled an impulse to pull a tallboy of Budweiser from the icy barrel next to the register. She was not going to drink today, despite last night's setback. She didn't want to fall into her bad habits. Her thoughts were like cars rushing down the highway in a video game and she was a frog, trying to hop across five lanes to safety. It took all her energy to not buy the beer.

As she walked toward the library she was feeling a mix of butterflies and bravado. She already had her speech planned out. She would give Marisol the flowers and ask her if there were any books on how to build miniature bird bicycles. She had considered buying her a blue lovebird she'd seen in the pet store window. "Need I say more?" she would say, setting the cage down on the checkout desk. When she'd told Sammy the idea she'd said maybe that was a bit much.

While she waited for the light to change Theo read the neon flyers taped to the light pole.

GET PAID TO DRINK ALCOHOL

Was God speaking to her directly? She tore off one of the bright pink strips, and one from the green flyer that simply said DEPRESSED?

It was like a work fair designed specifically for her.

"How was Atlantic City?" she heard someone say.

Marisol was standing next to her.

"Uh. Hi."

"Did you win money?"

"Actually yes," Theo said. "Here."

She handed Marisol the flowers. She took them, seeming a little stunned.

If possible, Marisol looked even hotter than Theo had remembered. She was wearing tight black jeans with knee-high black leather boots and a fitted black peacoat.

"I'm job hunting," Theo said, gesturing to the flyers.

"I should join you," Marisol said, pulling off a phone number for herself. "I just got laid off."

"What?"

Marisol nodded. "Right in time for Christmas."

"Fuck. That sucks."

Marisol ran her finger over the edge of the rose.

"Maybe you'd like to be in the depression study together," Theo said, excitedly.

Marisol just stood there holding the flowers. A cold wind had picked up and blown a few strands of her long hair into her lip gloss. She plucked at them.

"Can I buy you dinner? Or a drink? Or take you to Atlantic City? I'm considering becoming a professional gambler."

"Atlantic City sounds good," Marisol said.

"Really? I have a truck."

Marisol gave her a small smile.

"Or maybe you want to be alone?"

"I don't want to be alone," Marisol said.

"Okay. Wait here a second."

Marisol watched Theo run across the street and drop her library books through the return slot. She jogged back across the street, winded.

"I've got to quit smoking," Theo said, pulling a cigarette out of her pack.

"Do you want to go to the city?" Marisol said.

"Now?"

"Yeah. I feel like I ought to show you the real New York since you just moved here."

It had started to snow.

"Snow," Theo said, smiling.

"Wait till you live here awhile. It won't be so exciting."

Theo looped her arm through Marisol's and they walked to the subway with their heads bent down against the cold. On the train, Theo pulled out her copy of *Crime and Punishment*.

"You ever read this?"

"How weird. That actually used to be my favorite book."

"Why? I loved *The Gambler* and *Notes From the Underground*, but I can't seem to get into this one."

"I bet you loved *The Gambler*," Marisol teased. "Do you always call girls you just met from Atlantic City at 2 AM?"

"Only if I really like them."

Theo wanted to take Marisol's hand but she was cradling the flowers. Plus they were sharing the train with a boys' sports team, loudly shouting back and forth to each other.

By the time Marisol said, "This stop is ours" and grabbed her hand to get up, Theo was trying to figure out if she'd say yes or no if Marisol offered her a drink.

The subway station smelled like piss and wet wool coats. The combination of rush hour and the holidays made her feel like they were in a movie. When they emerged from the station onto the street, the air was filled with a sugary smell.

"What's that smell?" she asked Marisol.

"Nuts for nuts! Have you ever had them?"

"No."

Marisol led Theo to a food cart where a man was selling hot nuts.

"I'm a nut," Theo told him.

"What kind do you want?" Marisol asked.

"The peanuts," she said because they were familiar.

Marisol started to pay, but Theo stopped her.

"No," Theo said, retrieving the wad of cash from her pocket. "I won all this money."

Marisol just looked at her.

"You can't just get the peanuts," Marisol said.

"Can I try all of them?" Theo asked.

"I'm out of chestnuts," the nuts man said.

"I would love a job like this," Theo told Marisol. "Cary Grant could sleep on the ground next to me all day."

"Who's Cary Grant?" Marisol asked.

"My dog."

The man filled a waxed bag with warm candied cashews, peanuts and almonds, and handed it to her. Theo let the sugar coating on a single candied peanut dissolve on her tongue and then offered the bag to Marisol, who poured a few almonds into the palm of her hand and popped them in her mouth like they were pills.

"Do you like them?" Marisol asked.

Theo nodded happily. She felt like someone on the top of a holiday cookie tin, jovially trudging through snowdrifts, wearing a bright red winter hat and matching scarf, with perfect circles of red rouge on each of her cheeks. She took Marisol's hand and led her out of the crowd and up against the side of a building.

"Can I kiss you?" she asked.

But Marisol kissed her first, her mouth a mix of candied nuts and cigarettes. Theo pinned Marisol's body against the wall and they kissed a long time, until Theo felt drunk. She only worried fleetingly about getting bashed in the head with a crowbar for being gay. Finally, Marisol pulled away and led Theo back onto the crowded sidewalk. Everyone who passed them had arms filled with packages and bags preparing for Christmas. Theo offered Marisol more nuts.

"I've got a bad tooth," she said. The confidence Marisol had diplayed until then, mostly in a certain pursing of her lips, was gone now. She looked ashamed.

"Me too," Theo said. "I need my wisdom teeth pulled. My friend Big Vic told me Bellevue has a low-income dental clinic."

"Ooh, we could have a public hospital date after we have a romantic getaway as participants in the depression study," Marisol said. "Okay, stop here. You are about to witness some quintessential New York."

Below them was a crowded ice-skating rink.

"What's this?" Theo asked.

"Rockefeller Center."

Theo stared at Marisol. She wanted to kiss her again.

"You want to skate?" Marisol asked.

"Down there?"

The group of people gathered around the ice-skating rink suddenly let out a wild cheer.

"What just happened?" Theo asked.

"Someone fell. Everyone cheers when someone falls."

"That's nice," Theo said, smiling.

"Want to try it?"

"Okay."

Theo had only skated a couple of times in her life but decided to adopt a fearless attitude. Plus, she could use it as an excuse to hold Marisol's hand. If they kept moving then they were still on a date, and if they were still on a date then Theo was still the dapper gentleman with the long red scarf on top of the holiday cookie tin, the world a perfect place full of ice-skating butter-cookie eaters. The rink was packed with teenagers and excited children shrieking in delight at each fall. Theo wished Cary Grant was there, in her own double pair of ice-skates. After stiff-legging her way around the perimeter of the rink a few times she mustered up the courage to let go of the wall. Marisol was a natural—not doing anything too advanced like backward skating or loops, but gliding easily. Every once in a while she'd look back at Theo and laugh sweetly. Theo pushed off hard and dug into the ice, passing Marisol, and tried to bow like an old movie star, one arm across her body. Her feet tangled underneath her and she went facedown into the ice. She tasted blood and heard the crowd cheer wildly.

ten

Aside from a bloody lip, Theo was fine. On the subway ride home Marisol teased her about her skating skills and kissed the thin cut on her bottom lip. Theo felt as if all the happiness in the world were emanating from that cut. And while she kissed Marisol back, she didn't care that her lip hurt or that there might be a gaybasher lurking about.

"Do you want to get a drink?" Marisol asked as the train crossed from Manhattan into Brooklyn.

"Sure," Theo said, not wanting her date to end.

"Do you mind if we run by my place first? It's right off the subway."

"Is that a pickup line?" Marisol nodded, then pulled her off the N train at 59th Street and headed toward the door of Sammy's bar, The Looney Bin.

Joey wasn't outside.

"Are you taking me to The Looney Bin?" Theo asked.

"How do you know about The Looney Bin?"

"My roommate bartends there."

"Really?"

"I'm going to poke my head in and say hi to her," Theo said.

"I'll meet you in there. I'm just going to run upstairs," Marisol said.

It was slow inside The Looney Bin, and Joey was sitting at the end of the bar next to one of the dancers who was putting on makeup.

"Girl!" Sammy said, surprised. "What are you doing here?"

"I'm on a date with Marisol," Theo whispered. "She lives upstairs."

"Really?"

Theo nodded. Everyone in the bar was watching the news.

"Oh my God," Theo said, seeing the woman who'd won the three-million-dollar lotto. "She finally came forward."

"She's a high school teacher," Sammy said.

Theo watched a heavyset woman navigate through a crowd of reporters.

"The ticket was in her coat pocket," Sammy said.

Joey flipped through the channels with a remote, stopping at another news station. Sammy filled a glass with Coke, and Theo drank it while watching a story about an environmental group that had accused the Navy of dumping thousands of gallons of fuel into the ocean so their planes would be light enough to land on aircraft carriers.

"I can't wait till all this shit is done," said Candy, who'd come and stood next to Theo.

The first time Theo met Candy she was flirting with Sammy while wearing nothing but what appeared to be a single shoelace wrapped around her entire body. Candy was the only out queer stripper at The Looney Bin, and each night she got dropped off in a red Mustang convertible by her butch. They were doppelbangers—both with short bleached Afros—Candy's Afro femme to her girlfriend's butch.

"Can't wait till what's done?" Theo said lighting a cigarette, offering Candy one.

"Till it's all fucking over. The whole fucking thing. The whole fucking human race."

Sammy was pouring tequila shots for everyone sitting at the bar, sliding two toward Candy and Theo.

"You drinking, girl?" Sammy gestured to the tequila.

"I hate tequila," Theo said.

"Hi," Marisol came in and touched Theo on the arm.

"This is my friend Sammy," said Theo, introducing Marisol.

"Hi," Sammy said.

"Hello." Marisol shook Sammy's hand.

"What are you guys up to?" Sammy asked.

"We might go to Atlantic City," Theo said.

"Really? Two nights in a row? You should just move there."

"I got laid off today," Marisol said. "My schedule is pretty open."

"That sucks." Sammy poured a tequila shot for Marisol.

"Girl, you should work here. You could make mad money," Candy told Marisol.

"I wouldn't have a commute," Marisol said, clinking glasses with Candy before they both downed the shots.

"Joey," Candy called, "come here."

Joey kissed one of the strippers on the cheek, set down the remote and walked down to where Candy was.

"My girl here wants a little work, can you help her?"

Joey looked Marisol up and down.

"I know you, right?"

"I live in one of the apartments upstairs. I've passed you in the hallway before."

"You ever dance before?"

"No."

"What's your name?"

"She don't have a name yet, Joey," Candy interrupted.

Theo watched Marisol.

"Well we got a big party tomorrow. If you want to come in early Candy can show you the ropes."

"Thanks," Marisol said to Joey, who nodded and walked away.

"Girl, you can make some money here," Candy repeated before disappearing into the main room.

"Are you really going to work here?" Theo said.

"I don't know. I am unemployed. How hard could it be?"

"Well, I've gotta to get back to work. It was nice to meet you," Sammy said.

"Nice to meet you too," Marisol said.

"I'll see you later, Sammy," Theo said.

"I want to take you to this great underground place on 5th Avenue. It looks like a thrift store but it's a bar," Marisol said, grabbing Theo's hand.

Theo held onto Marisol's hand as they walked down the icy sidewalk back to the subway, telling herself she was only going to have a few drinks. They kept their heads down to shield their faces from the bitter cold. When they arrived at the "bar" Theo recognized it. She'd passed it the night she'd taken Sammy to lobster night and had been intrigued by the collection of clutter that filled the windows. You would never guess it was a bar from walking by. In the highest window Theo had seen a creepy cardboard box filled with blonde wigs and doll legs.

"This place is a bar?" she asked incredulously.

"Yeah, two feuding sisters own this place. And one operates it as a bar at night," Marisol said.

There was a sandwich board out front that said LIVE MUSIC $2 BEER (COLD). Theo guessed it was left over from summertime when cold beer would sound attractive. She held the door open for Marisol and they stepped inside, thankful to be out of the cold. The place looked like the warehouses that thrift stores use to sort through donations, a forest of disorganized clutter. Cabaret-style music played on a crackly record player set up in the corner. In the middle of the room four straight couples sat in children's chairs around a small makeshift stage where some musicians were setting up. "Want to grab us a seat? I'll get the first round," Theo said.

Theo enjoyed the custom of buying rounds. It filled her with inexpressible warmth. She loved the civility of a drink simply appearing in front of her, and she felt like a good person when she was the one who bought the round. Marisol procured two red plastic chairs as Theo approached one of the elderly sisters. Her shrunken body stood behind a bar stacked high with several broken candelabras. A small chalkboard behind her listed beer as the only option.

"Two beers," Theo said.

"You want two beers?" the woman asked, in a tone that sounded more like an accusation.

Theo nodded, and the old lady rummaged through a dingy yellow mop bucket filled with ice and finally came up empty-handed.

"I'm all out," she said bitterly. "If you want the beer you gotta hang on a minute. Do you want the beer?"

Theo nodded again, tentatively this time, and the old

lady crawled under the counter and disappeared out the front door. Theo looked over at Marisol, who was laughing. One of the young couples was making out in the corner.

"Where'd she go?" Marisol called to her.

"To the bodega next door to buy more beer," Theo guessed.

The cold from the walk was thawing and the bar felt special, like a magic room that opened behind a trick book-case. The old lady returned with a six-pack of Rheingold curled in each of her old paws. Theo watched her struggle to dig each beer a tiny home in the mop bucket's ice, leaving two on the bar in front of Theo.

"Four dollars," she said.

Theo paid and sat down beside Marisol. She noticed a faint scar above her left eyebrow. She loved Marisol's looks: the perfect mix of pretty and tough. She smiled at her as Marisol fiddled with the colored disks inside a Connect Four game. Then she leaned forward and kissed the scar.

"Where'd you get that scar?" she asked.

"That's second date talk."

"Technically, this is our second date. Right? If you count the paella party."

"No," Marisol said. "That doesn't count. What are your plans for Christmas?"

"I don't know. Sammy invited me to hang out with her aunt and her boyfriend. But that seems depressing. I was going to make Cary Grant a steak. What about you?"

Marisol shrugged, "Some of my friends invited me to P-town. I kind of hate the holidays."

"Me too," Theo said.

Marisol took a long swig from her beer and Theo surveyed the room. "I'll bet the landlords are dying to kick these women out," she said.

"Oh, yeah. Probably won't be long before this place is a Starbucks."

They clinked bottles and each took a long pull of beer.

"They live upstairs. They rent the whole building," Marisol said.

"How do you know all this?"

"Oh, if you live in Brooklyn your whole life you know things."

Theo tried to imagine if their apartment was as cluttered as the bar. She pictured the sisters sleeping side by side in two twin beds with some mangy cats walking over their faces in the night.

"How's your lip?" Marisol reached out to touch Theo's lip.

"This is the second time this year I've split it."

"Really?"

Theo nodded. "Last time was at a bar the night before I moved to New York."

She moved her legs under the tiny table until she felt her knees touch Marisol's. The band began to play. A folky-looking woman started crooning and plucking a banjo. It sounded nice, the way city kids pretending to know about country is nice. Theo moved her tiny red chair next to Marisol's. She was inspired by the straight couple in the corner.

"Can I kiss you with my fat lip?" she asked.

"Only if you stop asking permission."

She kissed Marisol, both of their tongues cold from the beer. Marisol pulled away and bit Theo's neck hard.

"Your hair smells good," Theo said.

The guitarist started to pluck a few chords checking to see if he was in tune, and the lead singer set down the banjo and picked up an accordion. Theo noticed they all had a piece of wheat hanging out of the corner of their mouths, and it made her hate them like she'd hated trust-fund kids she'd known in San Francisco, wearing mechanic jackets and trucker caps to look working-class. They even let their own WASPy names flit away while taking on country-bumpkin names like Shovel and Buck.

She picked up her beer to take another swig, but it was empty.

"Want another round?" she turned to Marisol.

"I still have half."

"Catch up," she said, getting up and walking back to the bar.

Theo noticed someone smoking in the corner and pulled a cigarette out of her pack. She patted her pockets for a lighter but they were empty.

"Can I get two beers?" she asked the old lady.

The woman paused, lighting a match with her trembling hands and reaching her long paw toward Theo to light her cigarette for her. Then she dug two more beers out of the mop bucket and set them on the bar.

"Four dollars."

Theo left a ten-dollar bill on the counter. She carried the beer back to their kiddy chairs and felt a surge of adrenaline when she looked at Marisol. She was done pathologizing everything. Life's pleasures were simple if you let them be: smoking, drinking, and falling in love.

"Are you trying to get me drunk?" Marisol asked.

"Yes."

"What's your dog's name again?"

"Cary Grant."

"That's cute."

She told Marisol the story of how she came to have Cary Grant.

"Oh my God," Marisol said. And then, "I've always wanted a dog."

The heat was cranked up high in the bar.

"Let's get out of here," Marisol said. "It's like a sauna."

When Theo stood up she felt a little dizzy and was afraid their date was coming to an end.

"Do you eat meat?" Marisol asked.

"If given the chance, I only eat meat," Theo smiled.

"Let's go pick up your dog and go to my house and I'll bake us a chicken."

Theo wondered if Marisol was too drunk to make a chicken.

"I love chicken," she said.

They hailed a taxi to Theo's place and the apartment was dark. Sammy was still at The Looney Bin. Cary Grant greeted Theo at the door, wagging wildly.

"Oh my God," Marisol said, kneeling to pet Cary Grant, but the dog shied away.

"It's okay," Theo said. "Come say hello."

But Cary Grant scurried away, peeking out from behind the door. They followed her into the kitchen.

"Oh my God, you have a bar in your house!" Marisol exclaimed, picking up the martini shaker.

"It's Sammy's," Theo explained.

"Make me a dirty martini," Marisol sat down on a stool.

Theo wondered if this meant she wasn't cooking them dinner. "Gin or vodka?" she said.

"Gin."

Theo poured the alcohol into the shaker with some ice and pulled a jar of olives from the fridge.

"Do you have any food?" Marisol asked.

"Only olives," Theo said, "and peanut butter."

She shook the martini and poured the alcohol into two glasses, handing one to Marisol, who ate the olive hungrily and took a sip.

"That shit's strong," she said.

Theo found herself scanning the corners of the room for mice.

"Let's go into the other room," she said, "the lighting in here kills me."

"Smooth," Marisol said sitting down on the edge of the bed.

"What?"

"Bringing me into a room where there's only a bed to sit on."

Marisol tried to lean back while holding her martini and spilled some of it on the comforter.

Theo sat down next to her, taking the glass from her hand. "Sammy's going to kill me if the bed smells like martinis."

"Wait. You guys sleep in the same bed?"

Theo nodded. "And Cary Grant, too."

"That's so gay. Hold this," Marisol said, handing Theo her glass.

She pulled her sweater off. Theo stared at her dark nipples through her sheer, purple bra.

"It's going to be like that?" Theo asked.

"We have to hurry up and have sex and fall in love so we can break up and move on."

Theo put both martinis on the linoleum and started to

kiss Marisol's stomach. Then she pulled down her bra and began to suck on one of her nipples. She could hear Cary Grant lapping water from her bowl in the kitchen and the hiss of the radiator. Marisol pushed Theo's mouth off her nipple.

"You okay?" Theo asked.

"Yeah," Marisol mumbled. She looked sick. "I don't normally drink this much."

Marisol's nostrils had begun to burn the way they did before she was going to vomit. She'd seen a tiny mint-green trash can when she'd first walked into the room but now she couldn't remember where. She mustered the energy to roll slightly over on her side and then she threw up a long stream of alcohol onto Theo's floor. Cary Grant wandered in and stood a few feet away, sniffing at the vomit.

Theo went into the kitchen and got a glass of water and a roll of paper towels. She handed Marisol the water and started to clean up the vomit.

"Are you okay?" she asked.

"Can you take me home?"

eleven

Marisol insisted Theo come home with her and bring Cary Grant. They could have a slumber party, and the next day Marisol would make them breakfast. But instead of crawling into bed when they got there, Marisol opened a bottle of wine and started pouring out her life story to Theo. Theo was afraid of how Marisol's face had changed since she'd been drinking. It was almost as if she'd become a different person.

Marisol's mother was Puerto Rican and her father was a white fag who survived the AIDS crisis only to shoot himself a few months ago. Both parents were alcoholics. Her mother had been in and out of prison and rehabs Marisol's entire life. Marisol studied hard, went to the library every day after school and lost herself in books. She'd been a waitress in high school but she hated small talk. She knew she'd need a job where little talking was necessary. She fantasized about filing alone all day in archives or, of course, the library. She would be happy to sit at the desk hitting cards with a scanner and helping people find books. Or when it was slow, reading the new books that came in. It turned out that her idea of what it would be like to be a librarian and the reality of it were slightly different.

She studied to be a rare books librarian, but there weren't many of those jobs. So she was a regular librarian, which in Brooklyn was really like working in a homeless shelter. As soon as the doors opened each morning the homeless poured in with their sacks and belongings, vying for the best spot to camp out for the day. Sometimes Marisol thought the only people who still read books were the homeless.

Each day when she walked to work she saw a man bundled in his cardboard fort trying to soak up a beam of winter sunshine. One day she noticed that he was reading James Baldwin's *Another Country*. She'd loved that book and all things Baldwin. She sat on the fire hydrant and watched him for a long time. He was a very black man with a thick beard and matted hair lying inside an army green sleeping bag. And around him was his cardboard fort. Behind him, the doorway he was sleeping in, a closed-up bar. On the old bar sign were two faded red cardinals.

From that day on she made it a point to bring him paperbacks from the free box. She'd set them beside him when he was asleep or leave them on his cardboard fort when he was gone. One time, she handed him a book directly. She didn't know what to say; the man stank unbelievably. She breathed through her mouth as she handed him *The Plague* by Camus. *The Stranger* had also been in the free box that day. Marisol had loved *The Stranger* when she first read it—had even named a car Meursault after it—and she wanted to give it to the homeless man, but it was much thinner than *The Plague* and she figured a homeless man needed a thin book as much as a thin sandwich. She looked into his wild, crazy eyes when she handed him *The Plague* and thought, *I should've brought him both books.*

After he took the book she walked away, feeling afraid of

a man she'd only ever seen reading books. When she was a block away she dipped into a store to look back and see if he was following her. Of course, he wasn't. The store sold moving supplies, things like printed stickers to label boxes that said: *kitchen, bathroom, living room, den, library,* and a bunch of names for rooms that Marisol was sure no one in this neighborhood had. She thought about labeling the homeless man's fort with stickers to separate the rooms. Then she walked home and cried for a long time alone in her apartment.

Why did some people live inside and some people outside, and people like her mother inside the outside, in prison or rehab, kept in a drawer "protected"—like a really sharp utensil you'd never want to cut yourself with. She was overcome with sadness.

After she found out her father had killed himself out in San Francisco, Marisol began collecting moving supplies. She wasn't sure where she would go; maybe she'd get out of Brooklyn or get a storage space, or just put all her belongings in boxes and label them with stickers from the moving store. Was this grief? She barely remembered her father. How could she even grieve someone she'd barely known?

Marisol showed Theo the one picture she had of her and her father and mother all in the same place. It was Christmas. There was her pale father with his big '70s moustache, and a floor full of presents. She'd kept the photo in a box most of her life and had pulled it out only a few times, most recently when her father died, and once ten years ago when she'd tried to go to therapy. The therapist had made her put the photo on the fridge and look at her young self. There were presents placed around her in a circle: a leash, a collar, bowls, and when she couldn't take it anymore, when she was shrieking and begging her father, he went out to the garage and got a little white puppy out of a cardboard box that he'd been hiding in the trunk of his car.

The therapist got a lot of mileage out of that one.

"Do you think it's responsible parenting to put a puppy in the trunk of a car?"

She'd named the puppy *Eggnot*, because that's what she thought her parents were drinking. Marisol found herself defending her father; it was a big trunk and the puppy was fine. Warm and squirmy and so eager to sleep beside Marisol in her bed. A few months later, her mother made her give the puppy away. She got pissed when it gnawed some shoes and peed on the floor.

"And did puppy things?" the therapist prompted.

She'd quit therapy when her therapist suggested she go to AA.

Marisol had become obsessed with taking care of the homeless man after her father died. When word started circulating around the library that some of the librarians were getting pink slips her first thought was *I'm not going to be able to bring him any more books from the free box.* In Brooklyn people often put their pizza boxes, pink bakery boxes or Chinese take-out containers filled with leftovers on top of trash cans so homeless people wouldn't have to rummage, but Marisol's homeless man, as she'd come to think of him, was always eating overripe bananas and Marisol figured it was because he didn't have any teeth.

When I can't bring him books anymore I'll bring him overripe bananas, she thought. She began calling in sick so she could sleep all day. She hoped when she woke up the nothing feeling would be gone, but it lingered. She couldn't even cry. She just kept trying to start the day over by taking naps. Her family was like a species that was dying out. They needed to start over from scratch, crawl out of the ocean and grow some legs. But her father was dead and her mother was doing ten years for her part in an armed robbery of a pharmacy.

Eventually, Marisol passed out, and Theo slept behind her petting her head as she listened to her breathe. In the morning when she woke up, Marisol was cold to Theo, embarrassed to find reminders of her confessions from the night before. She stared at the photo of her father on the coffee table and then told Theo she needed some time to herself.

⋮

When Theo got home Sammy was shuffling around in her pajamas.

"Girl," Theo said, depressed.

"Girl," Sammy said, listening to her story from the night before.

"I love her," Theo sighed.

"You don't love her. You just met her. She's probably just embarrassed she got shit-faced and told you her life story. Don't worry. She'll probably call you before the end of the day."

"Will you go with me to Atlantic City?" Theo asked. "I just want to get out of town."

"Only if we go somewhere with a good buffet and you give me half of everything you win."

"Okay. We can get a room and take Cary Grant and spend the night."

"Somewhere with a hot tub?"

"Totally."

Sammy rolled a joint in the car and smoked it.

"Girl, I'm so fucking broke. You have to hit it big."

"I've been lucky lately," Theo said.

Even though she had five thousand dollars of her winnings left, Theo still felt pressured to win more. She needed money for retirement, after all. She didn't have a profession in the works like Sammy did with massage school and she didn't want to work shitty cashier jobs or continue her haphazard shifts as a janitor in the junk-mail factory.

"Do you know my father gambled away every single paycheck of my childhood?" Sammy told Theo.

"Does that mean you don't want to go?"

"No. I was just thinking about it. He didn't really bet in AC. He was more of an OTB kind of guy."

Theo felt guilty for a second for asking Sammy to come. But if something bad happened at the casino, if she fell into a losing streak, she didn't mind if Sammy saw her at her worst. Plus, she just wanted to escape, get out of town so she wouldn't torture herself about Marisol. If she won she'd help Sammy buy her expensive books for massage school, the kind with beautiful maps of the body, books where each page lifts away one layer of anatomy—first veins, then muscle, then bones. In a few seconds, the entire body disappears. Gambling was like that, too. A few pulls of the handle and everything would start dissolving: her confusion about a future with Marisol and the rest of the fears she carried around.

"I feel lucky," Theo said. She said the same thing at the start of every trip to a casino.

There were many intonations for this statement depending on how her life was going at the time.

"I feel lucky," like a runaway wife with a black eye on a Greyhound bus.

Or, like when a terrorist says to a hostage, "It's your lucky day." The hostage is given the choice to have his fingers cut off with either pliers or a hatchet. That kind of luck.

Or, I feel *real* lucky, her voice laden with disgust, heavy with the memory of what had happened at the casino last time. And then four or six or eight hours have gone by and Theo has lost all her money for the buffet, for even a hot dog or a cookie at the stand outside the casino doors, the vendor who sold sad snacks to destitute people waiting for the bus to take them far away from this hellish place.

But so far, she hadn't experienced that kind of bad luck since moving to New York.

Theo got them a room when they arrived at the casino and they immediately went to the buffet to feed Sammy's hummingbird metabolism. Theo was trying not to gobble her food and rush off to the slots, but once she was in the casino and could hear the sound of the machines it took everything in her power not to run off to them. In less than twenty minutes inside the casino all of her worries had morphed into a single problem—she just needed to find a slot machine where goats were surgeons and find up a way to line up five surgeon-goats in fifty-three different directions. If she could solve this simple problem she would be a very rich person.

Theo wanted to gamble in the smoking section even though Sammy was allergic to cigarette smoke. Deep down Theo couldn't really believe Sammy was allergic since she smoked weed every day.

"Are you getting a feeling from any of them?" she asked Sammy, pointing to the rows of slot machines.

Sammy sniffled.

"Girl, you know I'm no good at that." She refused to pick. She didn't want to be responsible if it didn't end up a winner.

Theo was getting antsy and finally said *This one*, just so she could compulsively start shoving money into something.

Sammy sat down at the slot machine next to her, but she wasn't playing.

"Start slow, girl. Start slow," Sammy coached, sniffling.

Theo fed a hundred-dollar bill into her slot machine and another hundred into the one Sammy was sitting in front of. She'd brought a thousand dollars down from the room

"No, girl," Sammy said. "I don't want to lose your money." Sammy had never had the terrible misfortune of winning in a casino.

"You have to think positively," Theo said, and Sammy started to play her slot machine but not with any conviction.

Neither one of them was doing well and before long they'd both lost a hundred dollars.

"Let's go to the hot tub," Sammy said.

"Let me just win back that two hundred dollars first."

She quickly lost another two hundred dollars. She could feel all her promises about buying Sammy's schoolbooks going out the window.

"What's your limit?" Sammy asked nervously.

"Two hundred more dollars," Theo lied, thinking about the envelope of money in their hotel room.

"Girl," Sammy said.

And the way she'd said it filled Theo with shame that she could flush money down the toilet so easily.

"Let's try this one," Theo said, stopping at a slot machine called Ice Age.

The object of the game was to have a seal slide across the ice a certain distance and activate another seal to pop out of an ice-fishing hole with money fish in his mouth. When the money fish seal pops out of the hole it giggles like a teenage girl. If the seals slide too far, they disappear right off the side of the video screen, giving a sad little wave good-bye. And sometimes they don't slide far enough, never reaching the ice hole. When this happens, they push themselves up with their dejected little seal shoulders and crawl back off the screen. Theo had to try with all her might to telepathically control the length of each seal's slide. A player's level of luck is determined by how many money fish the seal tosses, and the fish flip and squirm in the air with each of their cash values emblazoned in their sides. So far the only seals Theo had been lucky enough to get to pop out of an ice hole had been depressed and unmotivated, flipping malnourished fish with low monetary value.

"Girl, can you try Reiki on the machine?" Theo asked.

"I don't know, girl."

"But you just got an A on your test, girl. It's not like it could hurt."

If Sammy could hover her hands the right way over the slot machine, then maybe the seals would pop out of the ice hole like the story of the loaves and fishes in the Bible, a constant replenishing basket of money fish! She could see the fear in Sammy's face. She was afraid of doing anything wrong with the Reiki that would somehow prevent the seals from popping out of their money ice hole.

"Please," Theo pleaded.

Reluctantly Sammy stood up from her stool and moved to Theo's left side, placing one hand on her shoulder and the other on the slot machine. Theo kept pushing the SPIN button while Sammy stood quietly with her eyes cast down, not closed, like she was meditating. If God is here come help us, Theo thought. SPIN. SPIN. SPIN. Her credits dwindled as the seals went about their day on the video screen, their bellies now full, and with no need to stop at the ice hole and pull out any fish. Maybe Reiki needed time to warm up—it was energy work, after all.

"Should I keep playing?" Theo asked Sammy.

Sammy nodded quietly and sniffled. Theo tried to imagine herself, Sammy, the money fish and God walking down the street with energy elbows linked. She took a deep breath and when she exhaled she felt the weight of Sammy's tiny hand on her shoulder, light like a bird foot. She knew Sammy's hand was acting as an energy conduit but she couldn't help but think it felt more like a foreshadowed consolation. Theo concentrated hard and pushed the SPIN button again. The seals had become like strangers in the subway passing her with their dead eyes. They had things to do, places to go. Theo'd get them.

"That's right, fuck you," she said angrily each time they went down the wrong hole, betraying her until each and every credit was gone. She pushed the SPIN button one more time to double-check that she was broke.

Sammy's eyes were open now and she stared at the video screen. Her face had the bereft expression of a TV surgeon who, despite repeated valiant attempts, loses the patient.

"Sorry, girl," she said, removing her little bird foot from Theo's shoulder. "I just remembered, Reiki only works on things that are alive."

"It's okay, girl," Theo said. "Thanks for trying."

"Can we go in the hot tub now?"

"Yeah," Theo said, cheerily. But she was already formulating her plan to keep on gambling.

twelve

Marisol had a terrible hangover. She wanted to spend the day in bed under the covers but she was terrified of falling into some sort of shame spiral about her blackout from the night before. She took a long shower and prepared herself for her first day of being a stripper. The fact that she'd known so many people who'd tried it at some point of her life, including her mother, demystified the job for her. Plus, now that she was unemployed she needed structure. Her drunken antics from the night before had proven that.

"Nice wig," Candy said when Marisol walked through the doors wearing a burgundy wig.

"Thanks," Marisol said, touching the tips of it.

She'd been a go-go girl for Halloween years before, and now she was glad she hadn't gotten rid of the wig, feeling some nervousness in her stomach as she looked around the empty bar, imagining it filled with partying men.

"Did you come up with a stage name?" Candy asked.

Marisol shrugged her shoulders.

"You need to pick one."

"I don't know," Marisol shrugged again.

"How about Chloe?"

"Okay," she said, feeling about as far away from a Chloe as a person could be.

"I'll show you where we get ready," Candy led Marisol into the back room. "Take this," she said, handing Marisol a tiny white pill.

"What is it?"

"It makes you feel like you're floating. You can just feel the music."

Marisol swallowed the pill and then had a moment of panic about taking something when she had no idea what it even was.

"Don't worry," Candy said, reading Marisol's thoughts. "It's just Xanax. Half of America is on it."

The back area was filled with women in G-strings, and Marisol let the Xanax move through her body. She felt less ashamed now about telling Theo her life story and throwing up on her floor. She wondered if Theo would come in to the bar tonight, although she didn't see Sammy bartending.

In no time The Looney Bin filled up, and Marisol was surprised how easily the dancing came to her. At one point both she and Candy were dancing on the stage at the same time and Candy started grinding up against her. It made Marisol giggle. She appreciated Candy's friendliness; the other girls were chilly.

When a new group of girls got up on stage Candy took Marisol's hand and led her into the small bathroom where sometimes the men got blowjobs.

She pulled out a tiny plastic bag of white powder.

"Want some?" she said, placing a paper towel down on the back of the toilet and then pouring two lines.

"Cocaine?" Marisol asked.

Candy laughed. "You're kind of square, huh."

"No," Marisol defended, even though it was true that she'd never done cocaine in her life. She was so afraid of becoming her mother.

She watched Candy snort the line and then she followed suit, tasting the drug sprinkle down the back of her throat.

"You ever throw up on a first date?" she asked.

Candy was checking to make sure she didn't have any cocaine on her nostril, and she looked over at Marisol and smiled.

"I just got laid off from my job as a librarian."

"You were a librarian and now you're working here? That's just sad."

"It doesn't feel sad."

Candy reached out and grabbed Marisol's boob, squeezing it.

"That shit real?"

Marisol laughed, slapping Candy's hand off. She nodded.

"That pisses me off," said Candy, who was pretty flat-chested.

Marisol wanted to say, "But at least you have parents."

But she didn't know if Candy did have parents, so instead she said, "Perfect tits don't make you happy. Just like being rich doesn't."

"Oh, I wouldn't have no problem being happy if I had your tits," Candy said, "because then I would be rich!"

Someone knocked on the door.

"Let's get out of here," Candy said.

At the end of the night Joey brought some of the girls drinks while they were getting ready to leave. Candy asked Marisol if she could do her a favor and pick up a case of video equipment for her the next afternoon. She'd have to meet Candy's cousin Sean at the top of the subway stairs, get the case and bring it to The Looney Bin the next day. Candy had already told her The Looney Bin provided opportunities for advancement; some girls gave blowjobs in the bathroom and some did porn on the side. When Marisol hesitated, Candy added that if she didn't do it then her sister was going to get pissed at her because she'd have to watch her kid again. Marisol always zoned out when people talked about children.

"Please," Candy repeated.

It wasn't that she didn't want to do Candy a favor. It just felt like her life had become so confusing, and she was afraid to be pinned down with commitments in case she needed to take a nap.

"Okay, okay," Marisol answered.

"Thank you."

"Can you give me a few more of those pills?"

Candy looked at her.

"Just until I get my own."

"Here," Candy said handing her the bottle, "just don't pull no Marilyn Monroe on me."

"I won't."

"I'll tell Sean to meet you at the top of the subway stairs tomorrow at three."

⋮

The next day Marisol still hadn't heard from Theo. She lay on her couch eating Xanax and staring at the red digital numbers on the cable box atop the TV until it was 2:45. She grabbed her keys and walked down the stairs to the subway station. She was delighted to find her legs rubbery from the anxiety medication; it had been hard to know if the drugs were working while lying on the couch.

The man in the bodega who sold her overripe bananas saw her standing at the top of the subway stairs and waved to her. She gave him a half-hearted wave back. She didn't want to invite conversation. It was very sunny for such a cold day, and she turned to press her hands against the sun-warmed railing of the staircase. Many people will walk up those stairs, Marisol thought, but never my father or mother. Eventually a train arrived, and a cluster of people ambled up the staircase. She scanned their faces until she saw a teenage boy with a shaved head carrying a hard, gray plastic case. He caught her eye.

"Are you Chloe?" the boy asked.

Marisol nodded.

"I'm Sean," he said.

She was expecting someone sleazier-looking to be delivering a suitcase full of porn video equipment. He looked like an athlete, muscles developed everywhere. He was wearing a brown nylon sweat suit with a team name on it, like he'd just come from practice.

He wiggled out of the crowd and stood next to her. *Angelina* was tattooed on his neck in too tiny script. In a few years it would be blurred into nothing. Marisol started to grab for the suitcase.

"It's kind of heavy. I can help you carry it to your apartment if you want."

"That's okay," she said.

She caught a whiff of his cologne, she knew it—what was it? Something cheap from her childhood that the boys at school would wear. *Old Spice*, she thought, staring at the gold dollar-sign stud in his earlobe.

"You sure? I don't mind carrying it," he looked her right in the eye when he spoke to her. She liked his politeness. Or was it sexism? Surely he knew she worked with Candy. Marisol thought she should ask him if he wanted to get some garlic knots or a slice from the nearby pizza shop. How old did a person have to be to have those jutting neck muscles? She studied his polite smile to figure out if he was thinking of her as a porn actress or stripper, or someone of Candy's generation—an elder. A mother.

"Let me see how heavy this is," she said.

She reached her long rubbery arm down and grabbed the handle of the suitcase. It wasn't that heavy. Like a few weeks of neglected laundry with a full bottle of soap on top.

"It's not that heavy," she said smiling.

The smell of garlic knots wafted over from the pizza place. The combination of the pills and leaning against the sun-warmed railing had given Marisol a sense of hope she hadn't felt in a while. Now, standing next to polite Sean, she felt like she was on vacation from the numbness of the last few months.

"You want some garlic knots?" she said out of the blue.

The boy's eyebrows lifted.

"Or a slice? My treat."

"Nah," the boy smiled. "I'm straight."

But Marisol saw his eyes lying. No young man could resist garlic knots or a free slice of pizza.

"But it's such a great day for pizza," Marisol said.

He laughed. "Maybe another time. I have to go to practice," he said, looking down at this watch, "I'm late already."

"Oh."

"Nice to meet you," he turned to leave.

"Yeah, you too."

He hadn't called Marisol "ma'am," but he might as well have. She leaned against the railing and watched him descend the staircase. He was almost out of sight when she called "Thanks," and he looked back over his shoulder and smiled, giving her a little wave like the kind a boy gives their childhood friend when they part at the bus stop after school.

Marisol lugged the video case into the pizza shop and ordered a bag of garlic knots and a diet soda. The man behind the counter picked five garlic knots from a silver tray with a pair of tongs and dropped them into a white paper bag. She felt his eyes on her; she knew she got better customer service because of her looks. She slid the video case into a corner booth and scooted in next to it. She fished the prescription bottle out of her purse and shook two more of the tiny white pills into the palm of her hand. It had been so long since she'd felt like she was on vacation and she didn't want to lose that feeling. She popped one of the pills into her mouth and took a quick swig of diet soda; she loved its bitter flavor. She looked at the other pill and heard Candy's voice saying, "Don't pull no Marilyn Monroe on me."

As much as she wanted to swallow it so she could be on super vacation, she was afraid to take too many at once, lest she build up a tolerance.

The garlic knots were still warm. She bit into one, the butter and garlic coating her teeth. Garlic knots were vacation food. She should go to P-town and visit her friends. But did people vacation alone? Maybe only sad people who were pretending to be happy. She stretched her legs out under the table, imagining Sean was across from her and she was seducing him easily, touching his legs with hers, inching down the V in her T-shirt with her pinky finger. But really she wished Theo was there. Had she scared Theo away with her coldness? She finished the garlic knot and picked up another one.

"Goddammit!" the man behind the counter yelled. He was shaking an enormous tub of white shredded cheese into a smaller tub and watching a soccer game on TV.

He caught Marisol's eye and said, "Why do they want to break my heart?" gesturing to the TV, which was showing an instant replay of what Marisol assumed was the wrong team scoring a goal.

She smiled and went back to her garlic knot. Men shouting at sports on TV were not her idea of vacation.

"Every game, they make the same mistakes," he said.

"It always gets darkest right before it gets pitch black," Marisol replied.

"What's that?" the man asked, wiping his hands on his apron and turning the TV down with the remote. He'd finally succeeded in his plan to get her to talk to him.

She ignored him. She was his hostage, the only person in the shop. Soon the gaggle of high school kids would flood in from across the street and push each other and screech and order their slices. The thought made Marisol open her purse and retrieve one of the white pills. She threw it into a mouthful of diet soda like a person tosses a bottle with a message in it into a breaking wave, and swallowed. Then she folded the top of the paper bag down neatly, into perfect, symmetrical rectangles. She wanted to save a few garlic knots for later, and she wanted to escape the man behind the counter.

"I didn't hear you," he said as she slid out of the booth and walked toward the door, the video case now heavier in her hand.

She looked at him, puzzled.

"You just said something to me," he said, a touch angrily.

Marisol remembered, the soccer game.

"Oh," she smiled. Her rubber knees giggled underneath

her. She remembered the first time her mom came home from rehab talking about God's will.

"I said, 'We don't always know God's will.'"

He looked at her, incensed. "No, that's not what you said."

"It's what I *meant* to say."

She moved her hand over her cleavage, adjusting the V of her white T-shirt. She didn't need to will the man's eyes to follow her hand. They just did. *I should be a hypnotist*, she thought. *A titnotist!* She laughed at her little joke and smiled at the man. She thought about making jazz hands at him and saying, *A titnotist!* But she was still holding the video case.

"Do you know what's God's will? This," she said firmly, raising the bag of remaining garlic knots up so he could see them over the counter.

He frowned. She'd upset him. His God had nothing to do with garlic knots. She certainly wasn't going to waste the first day of her vacation fighting with this man about religion. She felt great, cradled and safe against the bosom of the tiny white pills. Or like a dog running free through the house, gobbling cat shit out of the litter box. The man looked a touch scared, like maybe he thought she was going to rob him after her dazzling camouflage tactics. No one likes it when the pretty girl with the perfect tits turns out to be crazy.

"You're not feeling well," he said.

"You're just jealous that I'm on vacation," Marisol laughed, walking out of the pizza shop into the wind.

She walked the few short blocks to her apartment, hurrying up the stairs to avoid anyone in The Looney Bin. She had to shove her key three times into the lock before she opened the door of her apartment, flopping down on the monstrosity that was her couch, which was long and gold and from the seventies. When she had first seen it, she hadn't been able to decide if it was amazing or hideous. She'd returned to the thrift store three times before she was willing to pay the hundred dollars for it. She set the video case down on the coffee table. Maybe she could nap for a few hours before she had to walk downstairs and start her shift. If she'd seduced Sean she would have asked him if he wanted to take a nap afterwards. Or better, if Theo was here. She couldn't believe she'd passed out before having sex with Theo the other night. It was so nice to take a nap after fucking on vacation. Especially when a sunbeam was falling just right on the bed.

She opened the video case, and a familiar smell wafted out that made her mouth water. She tried to put her finger on it. She'd smelled it at the library, like some kind of old metal typewriter. Each part of the video camera fit perfectly inside its matching indentation. Marisol loved compartments; sometimes she went to a south Indian restaurant just to get served on a metal tray that had tiny indentations for all its sauces. She pulled out the heavy camera with its black rectangular foam-covered microphone on top. She touched the foam, and was surprised by its coarseness. She ran her finger back and forth over it, like it was some kind of scab on her arm. She took the other attachments out of the case and placed them around her on the coffee table like an array of Christmas presents.

In the bottom of the case, hiding behind a battery pack, was a rolled up light blue dishtowel. She pulled on the edge of it, but it was stuck. She pulled harder, and as it unraveled she heard something fall to the floor with a thud.

"Oh shit," she said, looking at the small handgun.

⋮

Marisol felt her heart beating under her armpit as she leaned over and picked up the gun. She was afraid to touch it, especially after swallowing Xanax all day. How did a person know if a gun like this was loaded? In the movies, some dude usually jerked the handle down a few times quickly. She tried, timidly, but the handle didn't budge. She'd never held a gun before, and it was lighter than she'd thought it would be. She gave the handle another fruitless jerk and then gave up. Why was she using bad cop movies as a reference? She was a fucking librarian. She would just get up, put the gun in her purse, go to the building where she'd just been laid off and ask her fellow librarians if they could help her find out if the gun she'd accidentally found when she'd picked up a case of porn equipment for a friend named "Candy" who was teaching her how to strip was loaded.

There was a tiny button that Marisol assumed was the safety. She pushed on it, holding her breath, but it didn't move. Her heart was pounding. The room was thick with the smell of metal, her tongue even tasted metallic. She needed to get to the library before it closed to get the right book on how to load a gun. Her father had known how to load a gun. She didn't understand how people knew the right ways to kill themselves. Where exactly to shoot themselves in the head, how to tie a noose. Her throat tightened and she felt herself on the verge of tears. Since her father had died she'd let most of her friends drift away. Now she wished she had someone to call. Why didn't Theo call? She wished there were instant friends like instant soups. Someone you could call when you discovered guns. They just came over and you exchanged looks and smoked cigarettes and somehow figured it all out. She had a terrible desire to lick the barrel. She brought the barrel toward her face and looked into it, sniffing for the source of the smell of metal that had overtaken the room. It was pitch black inside the barrel. Staring into it, she thought maybe she saw an ocean there, like putting a conch shell to your ear, but instead of hearing she was seeing an enormous Xanax wave coming at her. She watched its perfect curl and felt it crash over her.

⋮

When Marisol woke up she felt like her brain had been replaced by the blue wadded up dishtowel that had been wrapped around the gun. Right before she woke up she'd been dreaming that the phone was ringing and ringing and ringing under a pile of comforters, and she kept moving the comforters to the side until she found that the phone was actually a frozen waffle. She was just having the realization that she'd gone her whole life not knowing waffles were phones when she pulled her creased face from the drool-soaked gold cushion and saw that her actual phone was ringing. Theo, Marisol hoped. She looked out the window over the fire escape and saw that it was dark outside. The phone stopped ringing before she could answer it. "Shit," she said and stumbled into the kitchen, a dehydration headache beginning to pound in her skull.

The refrigerator was filled with things that needed to be cooked. A chicken, some potatoes. A stick of butter. But nothing to drink. She shut the refrigerator door and the phone began to ring again.

"Hello," she said, not recognizing her own voice.

"Chloe?"

She almost said, "No, it's Marisol," but then she remembered the girls from The Looney Bin knew her as Chloe.

"Yeah?"

"It's Candy. You didn't come to work."

Marisol struggled to understand what that meant.

"Are you there?" Candy asked.

"What time is it?"

"Three."

Marisol tried to do some quick math. It had been about 3 PM when she'd gotten home from the pizza place. Twelve hours had passed?

"You drunk?" Candy said.

"No," Marisol said defensively. She caught herself and said, "I think I'm getting sick. I fell asleep."

She pulled a coffee cup from the cupboard and filled it with tap water.

"Sean said he gave you the video camera."

"Oh, shit. The video camera. Sorry."

"Can I come upstairs and get it?"

"I'll put some clothes on and meet you downstairs."

"You sure?"

"Yeah, I need to go out for milk anyway."

Marisol hurried, trying to put the camera pieces into their respective indentations. She didn't know what to do about the gun. Suddenly she felt guilty, as if she'd created this problem. She shoved it under a couch cushion.

Outside it was cold. Marisol glanced at the metal gate pulled across the pizza shop. Candy was sitting in the passenger seat of her girlfriend's car, which sat idling at the curb. She rolled down the window, and Marisol awkwardly handed the video case through to her.

"Thanks," Candy said. "You coming to work tomorrow?"

"Yeah."

"Good 'cause we got hella Christmas parties coming in."

"See you tomorrow."

Candy said something to her girlfriend and the car screeched off. Marisol walked two blocks to the 24-hour bodega. The man behind the counter woke up when she came in.

"Hi," Marisol said, and he gave her a tired smile.

She picked up two packages of crumb donuts and a gallon jug of Hi-C.

"That it?" he asked.

"Yeah. Unless you have any empty boxes."

He looked at her, not understanding. She almost said *for moving* but she stopped herself.

"I want to give some things to charity," she heard herself say.

"You need strong boxes?"

"Yes. Strong boxes," she repeated.

He nodded, putting his burning cigarette in the ashtray and wandering to a tiny door in the back of the bodega. Marisol heard him rustling around in the closet until he came back with a few folded-up pieces of cardboard.

"These are strong boxes," he said.

"Thank you," Marisol smiled.

She looked at the shelf behind the counter where rat traps, tampons, pencils and packing tape were displayed.

"I'll get some of that tape, too," she said.

He reached for it twice before successfully grabbing it.

She wanted to tell the man her father had died, but she knew she shouldn't.

She paid him, and he handed her the change and said, "Every day I have lots of strong boxes."

"Good to know," Marisol said. "Goodnight."

She walked home smiling, with the folded boxes under one arm and her bag of donuts and Hi-C in the other.

Everything seemed surreal, the way things feel after falling asleep in the middle of the afternoon and waking up at night hungover. Her apartment felt like a sauna when she walked in, making her dizzy. She laid the boxes on the floor wondering what she should pack first and then turned on the television, flipping through the channels. She watched the news and twisted the plastic cap off the Hi-C, taking a big swig. It felt so good to drink something. Then she took another gulp and shoved a crumb donut into her mouth. It was stale but she didn't care. The whole reason she chose the crumb donuts was because the crumbs distracted from the staleness.

⋮

Marisol had two plans. Plan A was to pack up her apartment, put her stuff in storage, drive to the parking lot under the Verrazzano bridge and pull the trigger on the gun she'd found. Maybe it was God's will she should kill herself, otherwise she never would've found it. Plan B was, for now, anything but Plan A. Since she'd found the gun three days had passed, and she'd stalled: setting it beside her at the kitchen table while she drank her coffee, on the nightstand while she read a book, on the coffee table while she painted her nails. It was like a pet cat that she coaxed to follow her from room to room through the apartment. The good kind of cat that never shed and wasn't too needy, and wouldn't lie on top of her in the middle of a New York summer heat wave.

She didn't go back to The Looney Bin because she wanted to keep the gun with her and she didn't trust the other girls not to go through her purse. What if Candy saw it in there? Half those girls carried weapons, afraid of creeps or stalkers. Still, Marisol was afraid they'd see hers and know it was a friend, not protection.

On the fourth day she no longer enjoyed threatening herself with the gun and just found it pathetic that she hadn't had the guts to pull the trigger. People who want to kill themselves get the shit done. Like her father. The police had found a receipt on his kitchen table for some stationery he'd bought to write out his suicide notes. The time and date printed on it showed that he'd bought it just hours before he pulled the trigger.

On the fifth day, Marisol decided to bring the gun to the police station as part of their no questions asked, get guns off the street program. For each gun turned in, a person got $75. She walked up to the police officer drinking a cup of coffee behind the thick glass window.

"Hi," she said.

"Hello."

"I found a gun that I want to turn in. I'm going to take it out of my purse, so don't shoot me."

He chuckled and knocked on the window separating them. "Bullet proof," he said.

Marisol put the gun into a little box the officer slid open for her, then pulled to his side of the window. He took a look at it and then at Marisol.

"You found this?"

"She nodded."

"Where?"

"I thought this was no questions asked."

"This isn't a real gun. It's a fake."

"What?"

"Like a movie prop. I can't give you any money for this," the police officer said. "But it's still great you brought it in, because stores get robbed all the time with these because they look so real."

Marisol let out a deep sigh. She couldn't even find the words to say good-bye. She had been ready to kill herself with a fake gun. She walked out of the police station and back onto the cold street. On the way home she bought a bottle of red wine.

When she got back to her apartment she poured herself a glass of wine and sat down on the couch, toasting to her mother and her dead father. Her toothache had progressed over the past week and she swirled each sip of wine over her sore tooth, pretending it was anesthesia, until the bottle was gone.

thirteen

With the exception of the cash she'd left behind in Brooklyn, Theo had lost all of her money while Sammy was asleep in the motel room. She counted and recounted in her head, realizing she'd lost over four thousand dollars. And her only current employment was as a janitor in the junk-mail factory, so that was like losing ten million dollars. On the ride home Sammy assured her that it was okay, but she wasn't really being honest about how much she'd lost.

When Sammy went to massage school the next day, Theo wrapped the Christmas presents she'd ordered before they left for Atlantic City. She'd bought two bones, a red plaid coat and a squeaky lobster for Cary Grant, and a travel massage table for Sammy. The massage table was delivered in a giant cardboard box, unassembled, and Theo dragged it across the shitty linoleum into the kitchen where she leaned it up against the bar. She put Cary Grant's presents on the bar under a miniature Christmas tree. Then she felt the terrible depression overtake her. She wanted to call Marisol, but it had been almost a week since their failed date. She pulled the scraps of paper out of her pocket with the phone numbers for the alcohol and depression studies and dialed the number for the alcohol study first. When the phone screener answered, it occurred to Theo that she didn't know if she was supposed to present herself as an alcoholic or a normal drinker.

"How many drinks do you consume in an average week?"

"Three," Theo said.

"Do you ever use alcohol as a tool to alter your mood?"

"No. Not really."

"Are you currently on any medication for depression?"

"No."

Because it wasn't obvious from the questions what population the study was serving, Theo answered each of them in a tone she hoped made her sound like a peppy sorority girl; sorority girls seemed to get things in life. She imagined the alcohol being served in a sterile, fluorescent-lit room. If given a choice, Theo didn't want to drink whiskey, rum, vodka or rubbing alcohol. She would prefer gin and tonics, beer, red wine or even Campari. Maybe she would meet someone and have an affair with another participant. She knew that people hooked up during these studies. What if Marisol could be in the study too? Then they could have some concentrated time together. When she hung up she had a bad feeling she wasn't going to be picked, even though they hadn't given her a flat-out no.

The real cash cow was in donating eggs, but when Theo's eggs had been young enough for her to do this, she'd been afraid. Even for five thousand dollars, she didn't like the idea of her genetic child roaming the world without her help. She thought she'd want to be there if the child were ever mired in depression. Now that she was too old to sell her eggs, she'd do it in a second.

When she'd moved to San Francisco there was a whole population of lesbians who made their living doing research studies, or pawning their eggs off to infertile suburban couples. A few had even been surrogates. Most were crazy self-mutilating heroin addicts who bought "nice" thrift-store outfits in an attempt to convince the straight couples, but the couples were as desperate for a baby as the lesbians were for cash. They would coach each other through fake interviews while drinking tallboys.

When asked *Do you come from a long line of taxi drivers and hairdressers?* the answer is *no.* When asked *Are your parents and grandparents college graduates?* the answer is *yes.* And, *no, no, no* to whether anybody's gay or mentally ill. Wear long sleeves. Dye your hair a normal color. Wash those dark circles out from under your eyes, crack a tallboy and fantasize about how you'll spend the money. It was like a bad B movie, throngs of zombie lesbian egg donors, covered in tattoos and track marks and self-mutilation scars, pushing strollers full of empty beer bottles to the hospitals saying, "We'll produce great offspring. We promise."

Theo took a deep breath and dialed Marisol's number. She would ask her if she wanted to go on a road trip to Atlantic City and she would win back the money she had lost. Marisol's phone rang and rang, never picking up with an answering machine. She dialed again, wondering if she had punched in the wrong numbers. When no one answered the second time, she gave up. She could see Cary Grant in the kitchen sniffing around the bar where the bone was.

"That's for later," she called out to the dog.

She dialed the number for the depression study, confident that if she could make it into any study, this was the one. Her entire life had prepared her for the job title of Depressed, and she had the references to prove it. The phone was answered by a very young research assistant who squeakily asked Theo a series of questions about her depression. Unlike the alcohol study, where she wasn't sure how alcoholic they wanted their participants, Theo knew a depression study would want her to bring all her sad sacks to the table.

"Is your sleep ever affected by depression?"

"No, I sleep like a baby. Once I slept through a fire and I didn't even wake up when robbers sawed my upstairs neighbor's door in half with a chain saw."

"How would you say depression affects your relationships?"

"It's nice because I'd never date someone who isn't depressed, too. It gives us something to talk about and allows us lots of time in bed."

"Are you on any medication for depression?"

"Nope. Au naturel."

"Okay. Are you currently employed?"

"Yes."

"What is your current job?"

"I'm a professional gambler and sometimes work as a janitor in a junk-mail factory."

"Okay. Thank you for your interest but unfortunately you're ineligible for our study."

"What do you mean? I just told you I slept through a fire."

"We're looking for people who can't maintain employment."

"But that's not fair."

"I'm sorry," the screener said cheerfully.

"This is really fucked up," Theo heard herself say. "You know more people commit suicide during the holidays than any other time of year and you're just going to tell people during the Christmas season they can't be in the depression study because they manage to go to work?"

She slammed the phone down, heartbroken, and Cary Grant darted into the other room.

"I can't be in the depression study because I come from a certain kind of working-class lineage that's made me always have a job. What if I was so depressed during all of my jobs that I showed up drunk or slipped away mid-shift to cut myself in the bathroom? What if I used all my sick days calling in because midway on my commute I felt the top of my head detach and float away in an anxiety attack? Do you need me on the couch reading Sylvia Plath or endlessly watching *The Price Is Right* while eating one frozen dinner after the next?, well, I've done that too, just on my days off."

"Should I shoot my fucking dog?" she wanted to call the woman back and scream into the phone. "Should I just get out a gun and shoot my dog in the head?"

Countless studies had been done about how living with a dog combats depression. The many tasks required to take care of a dog can help a depressed person remain active. At least three times a day a person has to walk a dog and therefore move their depressed body and get fresh air and take the chance of seeing a cherry tree in blossom or feel a sunbeam coming down onto their head, allowing themselves the window of hope.

Theo was sure all the slots in the depression study had been filled by cat people. Cat people can lie in bed all day if they want to, folding their depression close to their chests and then rolling over and keeping it locked inside the comforter. Cat people never have to put a leash on a cat and walk it. Only the truly insane walked cats on leashes. Cat people don't ever have to leave the house because of the greatest depression-enabling invention ever: the litter box. They can fill a kiddy pool with litter and plunk it down in the middle of their kitchen floor and a month can go by.

Maybe if she had a doggy door she could get away with her depression—just lie in bed urinating on herself as the dog ran in and out. Theo had never trusted people with doggy doors.

"I'm trying to get better," she wanted to scream at the phone screener. "I'm trying to help myself!"

Theo started to cry. Why hadn't she asked to talk to the manager?

⋮

Theo wished someone had told her to beware of sliding-scale therapists that slide too low. Then she could've avoided that five-dollar-an-hour-ex-postal-worker-piece-of-shit-therapist in San Francisco.

"Why are you here today?" she asked when Theo came in.

"I'm depressed."

The truth was that Theo had been depressed forever, but she'd become especially unraveled when she'd tried to quit drinking a few months ago.

The therapist blinked a few times slowly and said, "Depressed, huh?"

But she said it in this faraway voice, like it was she who was the most depressed person in the world. For the rest of the intake she made small talk as Theo sat awkwardly across from her like a stranger at a bus stop. When she left the office Theo had the same bad feeling she'd had when she'd left the offices of the thirty-three lousy sliding-scale therapists before her. Only desperation, poverty and ridiculous hope led her back to the office the next week.

"I saw this in the paper, and it made me think of you," the therapist said, showing Theo a tiny rectangular newspaper clipping the size of a personal ad.

When Theo reached to take it she pulled it back, saying, "Let me read it to you out loud."

Her taupe armchair faced Theo's taupe armchair, and Theo watched the therapist's frosted-and-tipped hair bobbing up and down as she read aloud.

"The Depression Van is coming to San Francisco! It will be parked in front of 700 Market Street from 5 PM to 9 PM every Wednesday in January to provide free screenings for depression. No appointment necessary."

The therapist blinked a few times quickly and then handed Theo the clipping.

Theo took it.

"I think this is for people who don't know they're depressed," she said.

The therapist sat silent, blinking.

Theo continued to break it down for her. "The Depression Van helps people find out if they're depressed. I already know I'm depressed," she said, trying to hand back the clipping. It hung wilted between Theo's fingertips—a piece of trash neither wanted to touch.

"Well, you can keep that in case you ever need it," the therapist said.

"If I needed it in the future that would mean I'd forgotten I was depressed, which in turn would mean I was cured," Theo thought.

"Tell me a little bit about your depression," the therapist said.

This was the first normal thing she'd said. Theo took a deep breath and started to relate her psychotherapy history.

About three minutes in the therapist interrupted and began to read aloud from a self-help book she had in her lap. Each time Theo began to talk she interrupted, saying, "Oh, hang on a second. I read something in my book about that."

She flipped through the pages looking for a passage while Theo sat, courteously enraged, watching the fog hovering over the hills through the small window behind her. It occurred to Theo that if she dove out the window and fell three stories to her death it would probably stop her from becoming a therapist, and that could be a help to others.

During Theo's third appointment the therapist said, "Tell me again, what do you do for work?"

Theo wanted to say, "I can't remember what you do either." But instead she said, "I'm a cashier, but it's my dream to teach ESL."

"ESL?"

"English as a Second Language."

"Huh?" she blinked.

"You help immigrants learn English so they can get jobs and housing and—"

"Oh, yeah, yeah," she said, disgusted. "Those people always came into the post office. 'Me no speak, English. Me no speak English.' But they always knew how to count the money."

Theo wasn't sure how long she sat frozen in her taupe chair before she excused herself to go to the restroom. She walked down the hall past the bathrooms, into the elevator and out into the foggy day to begin the two-mile march home. So this was five-dollar therapy. She could've done better driving four hours to Reno and feeding a five-dollar bill into a psychotherapy-themed slot machine called *Bonkers!* Get three psychotherapist couches in a row and you win. *Freud, Freud, Freud! You're rich!*

⋮

Theo tried Marisol's number again. This time she picked up.

"Hello?"

"It's Theo. Do you remember me?"

"Yes," Marisol said.

"What are you doing for Christmas?"

"Nothing."

"Do you want to make me dinner and then we'll go to Atlantic City?"

"Is Cary Grant coming?"

"Are you making a specific request?"

"I'm only going if Cary Grant is going."

"Let me ask her. Hang on." Theo turned to Cary Grant, "Do you want to go over to Marisol's for dinner and then go to Atlantic City?" The dog wagged.

"Well?" Marisol asked.

"She wagged."

"That sounds like a yes."

There was a silence on the phone between them and then Marisol said, "I was hoping you would call."

Theo felt her heart soften. "I've been working a lot," she said, referring to her all-night gambling bender in Atlantic City.

"What's Sammy doing tonight for Christmas Eve?"

"She's hanging out with her family the next couple days. She invited me but they're all allergic to dogs, and I don't want to spend Christmas without Cary Grant."

"Come over whenever you want," Marisol said.

"Okay. We'll come over after I go to the laundromat. Should I bring anything?"

"Just Cary Grant."

When Theo proposed the trip to Atlantic City she was imagining an expanse of time in the car to make out, some roadside sex, eating at the buffet and, of course, now that she was drinking again, a ton of free casino drinks. She took the remaining thousand dollars and folded the envelope of cash into her pocket. It was the last of her lucky Buttermilk money. She fantasized about putting the whole envelope of cash on black again and doubling it, getting on a roll like she had with Big Vic. She'd made a comeback once, why couldn't she do it again? If she made a whole lot she could give Marisol a thick wad of cash, help her out since she'd lost her job.

Theo went to the laundromat and then came home and got into the shower. After her shower she heard a squeaking in the kitchen behind the stove. There it was, a Christmas mouse, stuck to a glue trap.

She picked up the Styrofoam tray and watched the mouse's tiny black eyes glance at her face before looking away. Its back muscles quivered, struggling to move, but all four feet stayed planted in the glue. Theo followed the instructions from Bill the Exterminator and filled a bucket with water. The mouse seemed so afraid that Theo couldn't understand how this could be the more humane choice. She did exactly as Bill had told her, she lowered the tray into the bucket and as she did it she felt the tears come hot down her cheeks. How could she drown a mouse when she could barely go fishing with her father? She could only imagine every fish as a fish with a fish family. If she killed a fish, who would make dinner for the fish family or lead the conversation at the head of the fish dinner table? Theo was so overly sensitive to everything that she tried to feel nothing at all. But now it was impossible not to feel anything, standing in the freezing cold on the front stoop, sobbing in her boxer shorts, pretending not to notice her neighbors staring as they trudged by with last-minute Christmas presents.

How long was she supposed to hold the tray underwater to make sure the mouse was drowned? She'd read it so many times but she couldn't remember and was now confusing it with the time needed for boiling an egg. A tear ran all the way down her arm and looped around her wrist to where she was holding the tray under the water. Surely the mouse must be dead, because she felt dead herself. She lifted the tray, and when she looked into the mouse's wet face, it drew a deep breath. Theo thought the mouse had a prophet's face, and now she would have to try to kill the prophet mouse again. She lowered the tray into the bucket for the second time in a rage and held it underwater for a long, long time. And when she was sure there was no way the prophet could still be alive she left the tray floating in the bucket and went in the house to put on some pants. She thought for a second about whether she should bury the mouse in the backyard. She had killed a prophet on Christmas Eve. Instead, she got dressed and finished crying and blew her nose and put on a coat and lit a cigarette and returned outside, where she turned the bucket upside down and watched all the water run down the driveway. The tray lay upside down in a small puddle, and Theo picked it up with the mouse still affixed and threw it into the garbage.

⋮

By the time she was on her way to Marisol's, Theo had shaken most of the apocalyptic feelings she'd had from drowning the mouse and was beginning to feel excited. She popped into a bodega to pick up some wine. A bunch of men sat on milk crates, smoking and drinking and blaring Cuban music from a boom box. The back wall was plastered with posters of Cuba and Cuban flags. She grabbed two bottles of red wine and set them down next to the register. The man behind the counter was scratching a long loop of lottery scratch-offs and made Theo wait to pay until he finished scratching.

"Let me get two of those," Theo said, gesturing to the same tickets the man was scratching.

He ripped off two from the roll below the counter and rang her up. Theo pulled one of her hundred-dollar bills from her envelope and paid. Then she drove to Marisol's apartment with Cary Grant beside her.

They walked in the glass door and up the stairs to Marisol's apartment. Theo knocked, feeling incredibly nervous. Cary Grant sniffed at the chicken smell coming out from under the doorsill. She could hear Marisol walking to the door.

"Hello," Marisol said, giving Theo a quick glance and then leaning down very slowly to Cary Grant and saying, "Hello."

"It smells good in here," Theo said.

She hadn't had a home-cooked meal in so long. She and Sammy were used to eating slices next to the garbage can. Marisol's apartment was small, a studio on the second floor with a single window over the fire escape.

"Good," Marisol said quietly. "I bet you like chicken, too," she said to Cary Grant who'd trotted into the kitchen and was sniffing around.

Theo saw Marisol was drying the roses she'd given her.

"I gave you those," Theo said, pointing to the roses.

"Yep," Marisol said.

Theo handed Cary Grant one of her Christmas bones, and the dog took it and lay down in front of the radiator.

"I brought some wine and a lottery ticket for each of us,"

Theo said. "Let's scratch them now to see if we're going to be lucky when we get to Atlantic City."

They both scratched their tickets.

"Nothing," Marisol said.

"Me neither," Theo said, feeling vaguely superstitious that it was a sign of bad luck to come.

"How have you been?" she asked, trying to bridge the awkwardness.

"Good," Marisol answered. Neither of them mentioned their last date. "What did you do today?"

"Drowned a mouse. Did my laundry. Gave Sammy her present."

Marisol was cutting plantains.

"Do you like fried plantains?"

"Of course," Theo said.

She wanted to kiss Marisol, but after their last date they'd catapulted back into some shy dance with each other.

"Do you care if I smoke in here?" she asked.

"No. Just open the window."

Theo walked over to the small window and opened it, grabbing an ashtray off the ledge. She paused a second and then lit her cigarette, which trembled in her nervous fingers.

"You want one?" she asked.

"No, thanks. I'm just waiting on the potatoes. I know it's weird to have plantains and potatoes. You want some wine?"

Theo nodded her head, but said, "No."

Marisol smiled at the joke and then poured some wine into a juice glass and took a swallow. "Yes or no?" she said holding the bottle out to Theo.

"Not right now."

"Really?" Marisol said raising her eyebrows in faux intrigue.

"Crazy people go to laundromats on Christmas Eve," Theo said.

"Does that mean you're crazy too?"

Theo smiled. They were finding their stride with one another.

"When I went to put my clothes in the dryer this woman said, 'It's broken,' pointing to my dryer. There was an empty dryer underneath it, and when I went use that one, she shook her head. So I said, 'Is this one broken too?' And her English wasn't very good so she just said, 'Broken.' So I thanked her, because I hate when I put a bunch of money into a dryer and it turns out it's broken, and then you wait all that time and the clothes are still wet when you take them out."

"This is riveting," Marisol said, sitting down on the floor next to Cary Grant. "Isn't this riveting?" she cooed to the dog.

Cary Grant thumped her tail into the floor a few times happily.

"Anyway," Theo said. She took a drag of her cigarette and looked straight into Marisol's brown eyes, studying the scar over her eyebrow. She could feel her heart start beating faster and she knew they were going to sleep together. She could tell by the way Marisol was drinking the wine and teasing her.

"So I put my clothes in a different dryer and there's like a million TVs in this laundromat so I sit down and get some animal crackers from the vending machine, and on every TV is a breaking news story about that guy who went into his nursing school yesterday and shot up all his classmates."

"Oh my God!" Marisol interrupted, "Did you hear what he told the police when they asked him why he did it? Because he felt picked on and the school wouldn't give him his money back after he'd been kicked out."

"The whole point of life is to feel picked on. You don't see me shooting anyone," Theo said, and then, "but then I've never managed to finish school, either."

"It's never women who do shit like this," Marisol muttered. "Did you see his mug shot? Did you see his eyes?"

Theo nodded.

Marisol got up off the floor and came to sit at the window next to Theo.

"Why do crazy people always have crazy eyes?" she asked.

"It's true," Theo said, looking down at the toes of her new boots.

"Do you have crazy eyes?" Marisol tugged lightly on the collar of Theo's T-shirt.

"Probably," Theo said, meeting her hard stare.

Theo leaned forward and kissed her. She could taste the red wine on Marisol's tongue. Marisol pulled away after a minute.

"You do have kind of crazy eyes," she said.

"I love this scar," Theo traced the line above her eyebrow with her finger. "Is that fucked up that I think it's sexy?"

"Yes," Marisol said, touching it with her own fingers.

"Are you going to tell me how you got it?"

"On our third date."

Theo groaned. "I got rejected from the depression study today," she said.

Marisol ignored her and climbed into her lap. Theo traced the indentation in Marisol's throat with her finger.

"I was so pissed. They said they only took people who couldn't maintain employment."

Marisol tugged on Theo's earlobe a bit. "Sorry I threw up on our date the other night," she said, kissing her.

"Oh, it happens."

"How's your lip?" Marisol asked, touching Theo's lip with her finger.

"Fine. It's my wisdom teeth that have been killing me."

"I've had a toothache all week too. Maybe it means we're destined to be together."

Theo dropped her nose into Marisol's neck and inhaled her perfume. She could feel Marisol's heart beating. Marisol pulled the cigarette out of Theo's hand and took a drag.

"That's so disgusting," she said, blowing the smoke out of the corner of her mouth.

"I know."

Marisol squirmed out of Theo's arms walked into the kitchen, bending over to open the oven door and stab a potato with a fork. Theo watched her.

"Your ass is insane."

"It's true," Marisol smiled over her shoulder. "The potatoes are done."

Marisol pulled the pan of potatoes out of the oven and put it on top of the stove. Then she filled each plate with chicken, plantains, potatoes, spinach, and macaroni and cheese. Cary Grant looked up from where she was noisily chewing a bone in front of the radiator and watched Marisol.

"Do you want to hear the rest of the laundromat story?"

"No," Marisol said.

Theo started to get up but Marisol said, "Relax. What do you want to drink?"

"Do you have Coke?"

"No. Just wine and water."

"Water then," Theo said in a vaguely sorrowful voice, never wanting to commit to drinking a glass of water.

Marisol filled a glass with tap water and brought a plate

with only chicken on it over to Cary Grant on the floor. The dog looked at her a minute and then dove in. Then she handed Theo her plate.

"Did you cook all day?"

"I slept all day. Then I woke up and started cooking."

"Merry Christmas," Theo raised her glass of water in a toast.

"Merry Christmas."

Theo devoured the food. After every bite, she said, "This is the best chicken I've ever had. This is the best mac 'n' cheese I've ever had. These are the best roasted potatoes I've ever had."

Marisol smiled.

"This is the best tap water I've ever had."

It was true. The water had a sweetness to it. As soon as she started drinking she realized how thirsty she was. They finished dinner quietly, awkward with each other again.

"What do you want to do now?" Theo asked.

"I thought we were going to Atlantic City?"

"Do you really want to go?"

"Yeah. It sounds fun."

Marisol returned to Theo's lap with her wine. "You feel lucky?" she asked.

"In a few hours, we're going to be very rich."

⋮

They loaded Cary Grant into the truck and took off to Atlantic City.

"I wish we had a convertible," Marisol said, rolling down her window. She leaned her body out of the open window, and Theo put the heater on to combat the rush of freezing air. She passed the bottle of red wine to Theo who looked at her confused and said, "I can't drink that while I drive."

"You can have a sip, though. It's Christmas."

Theo took a slug of the wine and let it soak into her tongue for a second before swallowing. Relief went through her body.

"I wish there was a way for people to drive drunk and not get in accidents or hurt anyone," Theo said.

"Why don't you cure cancer while you're at it," Marisol said.

Being drunk in transit was one of Theo's favorite things: on subways, or buses, or cars—just something with a window so she could watch all that scenery going by. After she launched her mood ring for alcoholics she'd make an automatic pilot device that would steer a car safely if the driver was drunk.

"So what's your game?" Marisol asked.

Theo looked at her confused.

"At the casino?"

"Oh, I love roulette," Theo said. "Blackjack. Slots. Anything really, except craps. I don't understand craps."

"Did you bring a lot of money?"

Theo felt the outline of the envelope of money in her coat pocket. "Not really. What about you?"

"A hundred dollars," Marisol said. "And you know where I got it?"

Theo shook her head no.

"I worked one night at The Looney Bin."

"What?"

The Xanax Marisol had taken before Theo arrived had combined with the wine and she was flying. She told Theo the whole story of her night of stripping, and then finding the gun the next day. When she'd finished, she looked at Theo and said, "Now tell me a secret."

Theo looked over at Marisol. She was leaning heavily against the window, and she looked drunk.

"What kind of secret?"

"I don't care."

"The other day I was drunk and I let Cary Grant out into the yard to pee and I peed in the yard too so Cary Grant would feel like we were in the same pack."

"That doesn't even count as a secret," Marisol said. "That's like practically normal."

She put her hand on Theo's thigh. Theo scanned the side of the highway for a place to pull over to kiss her. She finally just pulled over on the shoulder and put the hazards on, making out until Cary Grant interrupted them by pawing at Marisol's shoulder. Theo sat there for a second feeling dizzy from their intense chemistry.

"Go win me some money," Marisol teased, and Theo pulled back onto the highway.

"Give me one more sip of wine," Theo said.

"No way," Marisol held the wine bottle just out of Theo's reach. She took a big gulp and then leaned in to kiss Theo, pushing the wine into her mouth. Theo pushed her back into her seat, swerving slightly on the highway.

When Theo turned to look at her next she saw that Marisol had begun to slide her jeans and underwear down. Soon she was sitting in the passenger seat, pantless.

"Tell me another secret. A real one," Marisol said, playing with her clit.

"This is the best Christmas ever. Take off your shirt, too."

Marisol undid her seatbelt and took off everything.

"It's fucking freezing," she said, and Theo cranked up the heat.

She resumed jerking off.

"You're gonna make me get in a fucking accident," Theo said happily.

"Toughen up," Marisol said, taking one of her fingers and putting it into Theo's mouth.

Theo sucked on her finger until Marisol pulled it away.

"You tell me a secret," Theo said.

Marisol was now kneeling on the passenger seat facing her. "My mom's in prison," she said.

"Really?"

"Yeah," Marisol said it like it was no big deal but the mood changed in the truck.

Theo wanted to ask why she was in prison but didn't.

Marisol started to put her clothes back on.

"You don't want to come?" Theo asked.

"You can finish the job later."

Theo smiled while Marisol got dressed.

They drove for a while in silence and then Theo said, "I lost four thousand dollars a few days ago."

Marisol looked over at her sleepily.

"That's my secret," Theo said, shrugging.

fourteen

There are doors that open onto patches of blue Caribbean. Theo had seen them in art movies. They symbolized escape and opportunity. That aqua hue that promises everything. Women could be these doorways. When Theo imagined bending Marisol over the hood of her truck and having sex with her, the rest of her problems disappeared.

When Theo and Marisol and Cary Grant checked into the simple motel room with two double beds in Atlantic City, it felt like they were on the run, it was something about the randomness of checking into a cheap motel on Christmas Eve.

"Look, Cary Grant. You get your own bed," Theo said patting the mattress.

Cary Grant looked around shyly and then jumped up. Marisol lay down next to the dog and hugged her. "I got a puppy for a Christmas once," she said.

Theo watched Marisol's sleepy face as she petted the dog's side. "Are you tired?" she said, trying to hide any disappointment that might be in her voice.

"A little bit," Marisol said, getting up and pouring wine into two flimsy plastic cups. "I know you probably won't believe me, but I don't usually drink this much."

"You're fine," Theo said.

"C'mon," Marisol said.

Every time Theo thought Marisol was too drunk or too out of it to be present she surprised her with some kind of lucidity.

"I shouldn't be drinking at all," Theo said, feeling the weight of the confession enter the room, but Marisol was nodding off and didn't seem to hear her.

"Candy gave me a bottle of Xanax," Marisol continued.

Theo listened, a bit afraid. "You shouldn't drink on Xanax," she started.

Theo had drunk on Xanax once when she was on a plane. She'd felt herself coming on to the pills while people were still boarding and putting their luggage into the overhead compartments. It was so hilarious how they tried to stuff their big suitcases into the tiny chambers and she tried to document the hilarity by taking pictures with a disposable camera. She took another Xanax, afraid of losing her good time, and then when the flight attendant pushed the drink cart up the narrow aisle she thought, *A beer sure would be nice right now.*

The next thing she knew she was being woken up by a flight attendant after everyone else had exited the plane. She was dying of thirst, and her disposable camera was missing.

Marisol pushed herself up with great effort and moved onto Theo's bed, lying down on her side. Her perfume brought back the dizziness Theo'd felt when they'd been all over each other in the truck.

"You're nice," Marisol said.

Theo slipped her hands under Marisol's shirt.

"In a perfect world," Marisol started, looking into Theo's

eyes, "people would just live out the rest of their lives feeling destroyed after a break up."

Now Theo could see her eyes, wild from pills and wine. "What?" she said.

"Like exes," Marisol said. "And my mother. They'd be destroyed, while I've moved on happily perusing a plethora of ass from a Costco-sized pussy counter. But sometimes there is no Costco pussy counter. Just a communist bread line, and when you reach the front, everything is gone."

Marisol laughed while Theo's stomach began to knot inside her. She wished she'd been drinking all night. She felt the terror of being sober while Marisol was in a blackout.

"Are you okay?" she asked.

"Yeah," Marisol said, mussing Theo's hair and smiling. Theo was relieved that she had logically answered a question.

Now Marisol was saying, "Put your fist inside me."

Theo grabbed the wine bottle off the nightstand and took a giant swig. The date had become a shitty, poorly built house being swept away in a storm. There went the corrugated tin roof.

She pushed Marisol onto her back and climbed on top of her, kissing her hard. She thought *as long as my tongue is in her mouth she can't say anything terrifying.* She felt Marisol wriggle underneath her, sliding her panties to the side. She took Theo's hand and pushed her fingers inside her. And then she pulled on Theo's wrist to push her fist inside.

"I want to do it on the floor," Marisol said and she crawled from the bed onto the floor with Theo's fist still inside her, and Theo fucked Marisol while listening to some kind of commotion outside the window in the parking lot. She could hear people talking and gathering and the sirens of a fire truck but she just kept fucking Marisol until she came, and after she did Theo slid her cramped hand out of her. She looked at Marisol's naked body and worried about how filthy the motel carpet must be.

"Come here," she said, dragging Marisol from the floor and into the bed. She pulled the blanket over her.

"We could live in this room forever," Marisol sighed.

"What do you mean?"

"I don't have a job anymore."

Theo thought about Sammy shuffling around their apartment alone if they never came back.

"Do you want to play blackjack?" Theo said. "Or eat a steak?"

She opened and closed her hand, imagining all the bones and tendons going back into their respective places after having been cramped inside Marisol.

"I'm tired."

"We won't need jobs if we win a million dollars," Theo said.

"I forgot to give you your Christmas present," Marisol mumbled. "It's in my purse."

Theo came in and out of remembering it was Christmas. She rummaged in Marisol's purse until she found a can of warm Coke next to the bottle of Xanax. Theo climbed into the bed behind Marisol and touched her naked stomach. The soda was warm and tasted extra sweet. Each time Theo took a sip, she felt some dribble down her chin. She wondered if Marisol was beginning to fall in love with her. Marisol had made her dinner. She'd taken her ice-skating and bought her a Coke. Could she include the Coke as evidence of Marisol's love? Theo moved closer and put her cheek against the side of Marisol's head where her hair was growing cold in the night. She hadn't realized how much she missed having a girlfriend until Marisol was there in her arms. She kissed her back a few times hoping she'd wake up, but Marisol was out cold. Then Theo panicked about the fact that she'd been drinking on pills, and she checked to make sure Marisol was still breathing. She was.

After a half hour of tossing and turning, Theo slid carefully out of bed and took the Xanax bottle out of Marisol's purse. She swallowed the tiny pill with a sip of warm Coke, pulled on her clothes, shoved the Xanax bottle into her pocket and went out to hit the casino. It was on the other side of the parking lot, and as Theo walked toward the entrance she could see a few people standing next to a fire truck. She remembered hearing the commotion when she was fisting Marisol.

"What's going on?" she asked a man who looked like a trucker.

"Car caught on fire."

"Oh," Theo said, already starting to walk away.

The casino was a throwback filled with taxidermied animals and slot machines that still coughed up coins instead of tickets. Theo watched a young fag cocktail waiter make his rounds. If she ordered a drink then she could go back to the motel room wild on Xanax and booze and make Marisol take care of her.

She sat down at a slot machine called *Wild Goose Chase*.

"Cocktails?" the fag asked her.

"Just seltzer," Theo said.

She set to work trying to line up geese who were wearing straitjackets. She tried to figure out what had made the geese go crazy, then scooted over to another slot machine called *Sheeploads of Fun*. She wasn't sure if she was coming on to the Xanax or what, but she was pretty sure that the sheep were prostitutes—happy hookers with hearts of gold. She willed the sheep hookers to line up in a row. The fag returned with Theo's seltzer and she pulled out a hundred-dollar bill for him.

"Merry Christmas," she said.

The fag looked at the hundred-dollar bill like he was going to start crying and that made Theo want to; instead she turned back to the slot machine and played until she'd lost her roll of nickels. Then she moved to the part of the casino that had newer slot machines, since she didn't want to be slowed down by putting in one coin at a time. She sat down at a machine called *Nurse Follies*, a slot machine based on the American health care system. On the second spin Theo got into the bonus round that featured paying a patient's bill. Each time she could benevolently pay a patient's bill she won more money. Finally, the bonus round ended and the machine said, *You have great insurance but it doesn't cover this.*

The combination of the Xanax and staring at the slot machines made Theo feel like she had mashed potatoes for a brain. She looked for a timid sirma'amsir slot machine where if you lined up three butch bathroom wigs you could win a million dollars.

⋮

Marisol woke up to Cary Grant licking her face and wagging her tail. She looked around the room and it took her a full thirty seconds to remember she was in Atlantic City. Her head felt terrible. The dog jumped off the bed and stood by the door needing to go out. Where was Theo? The clock on the nightstand said twelve, and she figured that meant it was noon. She got dressed and took Cary Grant for a walk in the parking lot so she could relieve herself, then returned to the room. She had no memory of the night before except her bad tooth was throbbing and she was sore in a way that she knew meant they'd fucked. Had they gone to Atlantic City but brought no luggage? She saw her purse on the ground and tried to piece together the night before. Her wallet was still there but the bottle of Xanax was gone. She felt panic at the thought of not being able to swallow a pill.

With much effort Marisol put on a pot of motel room coffee. When she opened the package of coffee Cary Grant looked at her hungrily.

"You want breakfast?" she said to the wagging dog. "Okay. Let me just get my head clear."

She hopped in the shower to wake herself up, then went into the casino to look for a restaurant where she could buy Cary Grant some breakfast. She scanned the rows of people at slot machines for Theo and then walked into a buffet where she filled a plate with sausage links and eggs and potatoes. When no one was looking she walked right back out through the casino holding the plate of food. She pulled one of the sausage links off the plate and tried to eat it but it made her nauseous. Part of her hoped that by the time she was back in the motel room with Cary Grant's breakfast Theo would be there. At the same time she couldn't imagine having a conversation with her head hurting this badly. Plus, she'd like to recover a few more memories of last night before she had to talk about it.

Cary Grant wagged happily when she opened the door, and Marisol patted her on the head. There was something perfect about how a dog greeted you. She set the plate down on the carpet and watched Cary Grant look over her shoulder and then devour everything. When there was nothing left she licked the plate completely clean and then looked up at Marisol.

"I forgot your coffee," she said to the dog, taking a sip of her own terrible motel coffee. She glanced at the plastic cups stained with red wine left on the nightstand.

The dog wagged then pawed at the door to go out.

"Oh, sorry," Marisol said, opening the door.

Cary Grant had diarrhea in the shrubbery and then raced back into the room. Marisol filled the empty ice bucket with tap water and put it on the floor. "You be a good girl," she told the dog, pulling on a hat, her hair still wet from the shower. She wrote Theo a note, placed it on the pillow and left.

She didn't know where she was going, but with no Xanax and no memories of the night before, she wanted to leave before Theo returned. She called a cab and took it to the bus station. There she boarded a bus and slept the entire way to Port Authority. She pushed herself through the throngs of excited people until she felt a bit dizzy. She bought a cup of hot chocolate with whipped cream from a cafe and sat down on a bench watching the numbers turn on the giant board, announcing the gates for each destination. When a new gate was announced Marisol would wait for the crowd of people looking at the board to disperse, rushing off to their respective departures. I'm free to go anywhere, she thought, but instead of feeling empowered, she felt lonely. She sat on the bench and took tiny sips of her hot chocolate, only what would slide through the square slit in the plastic lid. The first sip had been so hot it scalded her tongue, but now she let it—each time, she imagined the skin raising as if it had been cut by a very fine piece of glass, and her tongue was covered by those scars.

I'm going to finish this cup of hot chocolate and then look up at the board, and the first bus that catches my eye, I'll board, Marisol told herself.

She pulled the lid off the hot chocolate and stuck her finger inside the paper cup, fishing out a fingerful of stiff whipped cream. She wished Theo was beside her to share it. Theo would thank her and be grateful and eat it all and there would be this innocent quality to her face like when Marisol had watched her eat the candied peanuts. She hoped Theo was back in the motel room by now. Surely, Cary Grant would be needing to go out.

⋮

It was three in the afternoon by the time Theo got back to the motel room, and there was a note on her door to come to the office. She'd have to pay for another night since she'd missed checkout. She slid the key in the lock, and on the other side of the door Cary Grant was dancing nervously. She could smell the dog had had an accident.

"I'm so sorry," she said, quickly leashing the dog and taking it out to have diarrhea in the bushes.

How could it be 3 PM? Had she really been gambling for twelve hours? And where was Marisol? She returned to the room and saw a note on the pillow.

Theo, I gave Cary Grant some breakfast from the buffet and took the bus home. Merry Christmas.

Theo sat down on the bed and petted Cary Grant, who made a groaning noise as she lay down. Theo could barely remember the night before. Just that she'd taken a few of the pills and was playing the slot machines. She patted the envelope in her pocket and everything was gone but two hundred dollars. She pulled the prescription bottle out of her pocket, but it was empty. Then she rolled over, smothering her face in the pillow.

"Merry fucking Christmas," she told Cary Grant.

They were a pack of two, understanding each other's movements the same way a schizophrenic might interpret a personal message hidden inside the subtle movement of a cloud.

"I'll never let you down again," Theo told the dog, before passing out in the room that smelled like shit.

When Theo woke, Cary Grant was pawing at the motel door to go out, and she leapt up, trying to avoid another accident in the room. The dog got sick in the bushes again and Theo was surprised to see that the sky was dark. She had a throbbing dehydration headache and it felt like she'd been abducted by aliens or was in some weird sleep study, every twelve hours in a new reality.

She returned to the room and filled the last clean plastic cup with tap water, refilling it three times and each time drinking it all down. She didn't begin to know how she would clean the rug. And then she remembered she'd lost another eight hundred dollars. She took one of the hundred-dollar bills out of the envelope and put it on the nightstand for the housekeeper. Then she turned Marisol's note over and wrote, *To whoever has to clean this room, I'm so sorry.*

She dialed their apartment but the phone just rang. Then she dialed The Looney Bin but there was no answer there either. She didn't want Sammy to worry about her. Then she remembered Sammy was at her family's.

"I'll be right back," she promised Cary Grant, leaving the motel room.

She needed to eat. She'd hit the buffet then head back to Brooklyn on a full stomach and drive straight to Marisol's. But once she was in the casino she didn't even attempt to walk to the buffet. She went right back to the slot machines she'd been at the night before.

"Cocktails," she heard behind her, and when she looked it was the same fag she'd given a hundred dollars to the night before.

"Oh, hi," he said. "Seltzer?"

Theo nodded and gave him a small smile. She felt ashamed for still being in the casino.

She thought about the night she and Big Vic turned their luck around in Atlantic City. She had to think positively. She fed her last hundred-dollar bill into the bill feeder at the front of the slot machine.

"Scared money don't win," she whispered.

She read the fine print on the slot machine. A Royal Flush was 4,000 quarters with the maximum credits played. She tried to figure out how much 4,000 quarters was. Theo pushed the BET MAX button and then hit DEAL. The electronic cards flipped toward her. She had a whole lot of nothing. She hit the button again computing 4,000 quarters was a thousand dollars. So she would have to win the jackpot five times to win the money she'd lost in the last week.

The fag returned with her seltzer and Theo had nothing in her pocket to give him. He hovered for a second until Theo said, "Thanks."

She looked back at her screen she saw all King, Queen, Jack, ten, nine of hearts. The game suggested she keep the straight flush. She held them all.

"Double Down?" the computer screen blinked.

She'd won 1,000 quarters already but if she doubled

down she'd have the chance to win 2,000 quarters. She'd be dealt a single card and if that card was higher than the dealer's card she'd win. Theo hit the double down button. The dealer's card flipped over and revealed a ten of spades. The screen blinked and waited for Theo to push the DEAL button to reveal her card. She felt defeated. She'd only win if she got a jack or higher and wanted to prolong the agony that she'd just forfeited 1,000 quarters.

"Scared money don't win," she whispered to the slot machine and pushed the DEAL button with her other hand. Her card flipped and revealed a Queen of clubs.

"Yes!" Theo cried. She took a triumphant sip of her seltzer. She just had to get back in the groove. She'd won five hundred dollars.

"Congratulations! Double Down?" the screen said.

If she doubled down she would have 4,000 quarters or 1,000 dollars. That was the same as the jackpot. It's a sign, Theo thought, fueled with optimism. She closed her eyes and tapped the Double Down button on the screen. The house turned over a three of hearts. She couldn't believe her luck. There was only one card in the deck that stood between her and a thousand dollars. She touched her DEAL card and watched her own card turn over. King of diamonds.

She'd won a thousand dollars.

"Congratulations! Double Down again?" Theo's screen said.

She was hooked on the double down feature. It was like a slot machine inside a slot machine. A kind of exclusive country club game that Theo could only play if she'd already won.

"Last time, God," she said hitting the double down button again.

Her card was an eight of clubs. She paused a second

to light a cigarette and take a sip of her seltzer. She would either win two thousand dollars or lose one thousand dollars with a push of the button.

"Scared money don't win," she said, but she was already scared.

She pushed the deal button and the house turned over a nine of clubs. Theo sat there for a second and then cashed out her remaining credits. She was the pack leader. She had to get the pack home safely and she just wanted to be in Marisol's apartment eating fried plantains. She had forty dollars to her name and she went back to the motel room afraid that she'd been gone too long again.

Cary Grant came and pressed her body into Theo's legs.

"Hi," Theo said. "Should we get the fuck out of here?"

She left the motel key in the room and shut the door, loading Cary Grant into the truck. It wasn't until she was crossing the Verazzano Bridge that she remembered she'd left a hundred dollars on the nightstand.

⋮

When Sammy came home Theo told her the story of her Atlantic City trip.

"It's just money, girl," Sammy said, but no one believed it anymore when Sammy said this. "At least the good thing about having no money to your name is it makes it easier to get an appointment at Bellevue to get your teeth pulled. When are you going?"

"Tomorrow," Theo said.

"I'd go with you but I have school."

"I asked Marisol."

"Can she do it?"

"I don't know. I left a message. She still hasn't called me back."

"She's probably just embarrassed," Sammy said. "That sounds like it was kind of an intense date."

"You mean when I fisted her on the floor of a motel room while she was in a Xanax blackout and then left her alone for twelve hours while I lost eight hundred dollars?"

"Exactamundo. Give her a few days."

"It's been a few days."

"Give her a few more."

"Should I send her flowers? I know it's crazy but I really like her."

"You might need more than flowers at this point. You might need a skywriter."

Theo found the phone book and looked up SKYWRITERS in the Yellow Pages.

fifteen

Theo walked into Bellevue and followed a series of signs, hallways and elevators until she got to the dental clinic. She signed her name on a clipboard and looked for an open chair in the waiting room filled with sad-looking people sitting in bright orange chairs. The receptionist was behind a thick plastic window with a cartoon mousehole opening at the bottom where patients grabbed a blue pen tied to a long string. If Theo had been a Martian sent to Earth asked to report back about her findings of New York City, she would say it was a place where employed people sit behind clear bullet-proof plastic to avoid being shot by impatient people.

She took an open seat behind an older white woman with blonde curly hair and a rose tattooed on her wrist. She was probably in her forties but looked sixty and reminded Theo of someone in a crystal meth ad campaign. She once had seen a billboard with two thirty-year-old women side by side, one middle class and one homeless, the homeless woman looking a million years old. In addition to being an addict the woman also looked like a hooker. The street-corner kind. A street-walker. What an ugly phrase.

When Theo sat down the hooker turned around and

gave her a jovial smile. Theo acknowledged her, nodding. She didn't feel like talking to anyone and pulled *Crime and Punishment* out of her coat pocket. She caught a whiff of Marisol's perfume when she opened it. Then for the one-millionth time she opened it to page one. *On an exceptionally hot evening early in July . . .*

Marisol had been a stripper for a single night, which made her a sex worker. Sex worker had become such a liberal arts college phrase. If Theo could do a billboard series she'd photograph two women side by side holding *Crime and Punishment.* One woman would be the Bellevue streetwalker and the other, a recent graduate of Sarah Lawrence College with perfect teeth who'd done phone sex for a summer in order to write her thesis. Underneath would be text that said, *Which of These Women Married an Investment Banker?*

Even with her head bent down, Theo could feel the woman in front of her craning her neck and making obvious gestures to see what she was reading, so finally she gave up and held the book cover up so the streetwalker could see it. She wanted to stop thinking streetwalker in case the woman had ESP. She didn't want to hurt her feelings.

The woman smiled wide and read the title slowly, like a child: "Crime. And. Pun. Ish. Ment. That sounds about right."

Theo gave her a smile—the same kind she was sure many people had given her before moving past.

"Is that a book about this place?" the woman asked and then laughed wildly. "Because I've been waiting two hours for a root canal, so this sure feels like crime and punishment!"

She raised her pilled-out voice to say *two hours* as if by doing so she could aim it through the mousehole opening in the receptionist's window. Just then a police officer walked in and handcuffed a prisoner to an empty chair in the front of the room while he spoke to the receptionist. Everyone stared.

"Now, that's some crime and punishment," the hooker whispered to Theo, slapping the front of Theo's book like it was her knee. A few people stared. Theo was beginning to like the woman.

"This is where they take you if they can't fix your teeth at Rikers," the hooker whispered.

Theo watched one of the prisoner's pinky fingers twitch after being cuffed.

"I'm Daisy," she said, extending her hand.

"Theo," Theo said, shaking her hand.

The receptionist called Theo's name and she was buzzed through a heavy door. The clinic felt like a juvenile detention center, each door requiring a person to be buzzed in, and every piece of glass, unbreakable. A short Asian woman in a white smock led her down a hallway filled with rushing dental students in scrubs and into a room where Theo was instructed to sit down in a chair. The nurse reclined it until she was mostly lying down, and it reminded her of when she was sleeping in her truck after just arriving in Yonkers.

"I'm going to start your IV line now. You might want to look away," the nurse said. She slapped Theo's arm until a vein bulged, and Theo watched as she pushed the needle into her vein.

"I've never heard of pulling four wisdom teeth while a person's awake," Theo said.

"Oh, we do it all the time," the nurse said. "You won't feel a thing."

Theo gave her a skeptical smirk.

"You might *hear* some things," the nurse started.

Theo raised her eyebrows.

"Sometimes you can hear ripping or crunching if the tooth gets caught in the pliers or they have a hard time getting it out," the nurse continued. "Do you have any questions?"

Theo shook her head.

"Okay, we'll get this started in a few minutes."

"I look forward to hearing my teeth ripped out of my skull," Theo mumbled.

The nurse flipped a few switches, adjusted Theo's IV and left the room.

She waited in the cold room, wishing Marisol had been next to her when the nurse told her about the crushing sounds so they could exchange horrified looks. She was falling in love with Marisol, whether it was a good idea or not. She felt a pang of sadness that she wasn't there with her. She wanted to tell her the frog joke. The nurse came back into the room. Theo decided to tell the nurse the frog joke instead.

"How are you feeling?" she asked Theo.

"Kinda weird," Theo said.

"Oh that's good. That means the drugs are kicking in."

"Drugs?"

"We have some muscle relaxants running through your IV to get you ready for the surgery."

She thought it was crazy no one had told her they were putting drugs through her IV. That she was slightly sad and wanted to tell her frog joke made sense. She enjoyed the free drugs coursing through her veins. It felt like justice.

"Want to hear a joke?" she asked the nurse.

"Sure," the nurse said fiddling with Theo's IV.

Another nurse walked into the room and smiled at Theo before putting dental tools on a platter.

"Do you want to hear a joke?" Theo said to the new

nurse, who was chubby and had a mushroom haircut that reminded Theo of one of her high school English teachers.

"I love jokes," the new nurse said.

"Well," Theo started, "this frog walks into a bank and goes up to the teller and the teller has a nameplate that says, 'Patty Black.' And the frog says to the teller I'd like to take out a loan, I'd like to buy a new lily pad, but all I have for collateral is this pink porcelain unicorn."

The door opened again and a tall, black man with a shaved head, wearing aqua scrubs, walked over to Theo.

"Hello. I'm Dr. Jones," he said extending his hand to Theo. "I'm going to be taking care of you today."

Theo shook his hand.

"She was just in the middle of a joke," the older nurse said.

"You look like a model," Theo told Dr. Jones. "Your face is perfect."

He seemed surprised and then said, "The trick is a good moisturizer."

All the nurses laughed.

Oh my God, Theo thought, did I luck out and get a gay dentist?

When she smiled her chest felt tight, but she felt perfectly high from the muscle relaxants. She loved her new dental family. The only thing that could make it better was if she could have her teeth pulled with naked Marisol straddling her stomach.

"Let's finish that joke and the we'll get those teeth out," Dr. Jones said, smiling good-naturedly.

"You're a good person," she told him.

He smiled.

"You are," she insisted. "Because you work at the poor person's hospital. And because you have good person eyes."

"The frog was trying to get a loan," the nurses prompted Theo.

"Oh, right. Well, the frog gave Patty Black a pink porcelain unicorn and said 'I'd like to take out a loan for a lily pad but this is all I have for collateral. So Patty Black takes the unicorn and says to the frog, 'I need to ask my manager,' and goes back to her manager's office and whispers, 'Hey, there's this frog out here right now that wants to take out a loan for a new lily pad, but all he has for collateral is this pink, porcelain unicorn, what should I do?' and the manager says, 'It's a knick-knack Patty Black, give the frog a loan!'"

Everyone laughed and after a few minutes Dr. Jones lowered the mask over his face but Theo could see his eyes still smiling.

He leaned over Theo and said, "Ready to get started."

Theo watched him pick up the giant needle on the tray to numb her mouth.

"You're just going to feel a little pinch," Dr. Jones said.

She opened her mouth and felt him fiddle with her teeth, pressing on them with the latex fingers. When he leaned over she could smell his cologne—it was faint, like leather or a saddle. Then she felt the needle go into her gum.

"A couple more spots," Dr. Jones said, shooting the novacaine in.

Theo wanted to tell him how nice his cologne smelled. She tried to push her words past his prodding fingers.

"You smell good," she tried to say, but his fingers were still in her mouth.

"What's that?" Dr. Jones said removing his hand.

Theo paused a second trying to redistribute the saliva in her mouth.

"Your cologne smells good. Like leather. Or a saddle or something. I'm not hitting on you," Theo blurted. "I'm gay. As if you didn't already know that."

Everyone in the room became frozen. She watched Dr. Jones flick his good person eyes at the nurse who looked like Theo's high school English teacher and she walked out of the room. She waited for Dr. Jones to say, "I'm gay too!"

"We're gonna give you another couple minutes to let the drugs work and then I'll be back and we'll get those teeth out," he said.

"Okay," Theo said, ashamed.

The other nurse followed the doctor out of the room and Theo found herself alone and unbearably sad.

"Don't leave, please," she wanted to say.

Everyone was already gone and she was left in a room that smelled like dental fumes. Theo heard someone scream *FUCK YOU* so loud it penetrated the series of locked doors from here to the waiting room, and then she realized it was the streetwalker. She tried to stop the first tears from coming but she couldn't and then she began to sob into the thin paper covering her chair.

When Dr. Jones returned to a crying Theo, he nodded to the nurses and they flipped off all the machines.

He said to Theo, "We're going to do this a different day when we can put you all the way under."

"Please," Theo pleaded. "You have to pull them today."

The nurse looked at her sympathetically, but had removed Theo's IV and was now pressing a square of gauze where it had just been.

"I'm not crazy," Theo said, "I'm just in love."

The words fell out of her mouth pathetically. The nurse lifted Theo's fingers and pressed them into the gauze.

She didn't want them to think she was crazy and wheel her over to the other part of Bellevue that was a mental hospital. She wasn't crazy. The world was crazy. Who'd ever heard of handcuffing prisoners to dental office waiting room chairs?

⋮

A few hours later Theo woke up in a different room with nice Dr. Jones leaning over her. She was cold and her head felt hollow, like a scooped out gourd.

"It's the joker," Dr. Jones teased.

Theo looked into his good person eyes and felt her tears start welling up again.

"Sometimes I cry if I'm on drugs," she told him in a low voice.

"We gave you a lot of drugs," he said. "We thought you were going to calm down but you just kept telling more jokes. It's a knick-knack, Patty Black," the doctor chuckled.

She remembered telling the frog joke and cringed at what else she might've said. He sat down on a little black stool and rolled over to Theo's bedside.

"So we're going to send you home. And I'll give you this phone number here that is a direct line, so you're not on hold forever and tomorrow you can call and make an appointment. We'll put you all the way under with anesthesia and get those teeth out."

Theo nodded taking the card with the secret phone number on it.

"Do you have any questions?"

"No," Theo said.

"I'll see you real soon," Dr. Jones said, giving Theo's arm

a little squeeze. "And next time you come in I want to hear another joke."

"Thank you for being a good person," Theo said.

Theo was alone in the room. She walked over to a small, square mirror on the wall. She stared at her tiny pupils and then walked over to the sink to splash water on her face and smooth her hair. She wished one of Van Gogh's tiny brush-strokes of color were on this mirror and she could touch it. The first time she'd ever noticed the tiny brushstrokes, they had made her cry. Something about their smallness. She returned to the waiting room surprised to see the clinic was closed and no one was left. Marisol was sitting in same chair the prisoner had been handcuffed to. How long had Theo been passed out in the back room?

"Hi," Marisol said.

"Hi." Theo was in disbelief.

"I got your message."

"Sorry," Theo said. "I hope that wasn't presumptuous."

Marisol made a face. "The receptionist told me you had a bad reaction to the drugs."

"Did they say I was crazy?" Theo whispered.

Marisol smiled, shaking her head. They walked out of the clinic.

"This place, this place," Theo started.

Marisol took Theo's hand.

"You can't believe what I've seen today. It's like an apocalyptic novel. Prisoners handcuffed to seats."

Marisol's hand in her own and her presence in the waiting room melted away the post-drug despair.

"Everyone needs someone to walk through this despicable world with," Theo said to Marisol in the elevator, like a wedding proposal.

Holding Marisol's hand steadied her. It made her feel moored and solid, like new boots. When they reached the street, Theo was surprised to see it was still sunny.

"We should take a cab," Marisol said, hailing one.

Theo sat down on a fire hydrant and put her arms around Marisol's middle.

Theo wanted to say, "I need you," but instead said, "I think I had a nervous breakdown in there."

Marisol looked concerned as a cab screeched over to the sidewalk.

"We're going to Brooklyn," Marisol said.

"I told my frog joke."

"What frog joke?" Marisol asked.

"I'll tell you sometime," Theo said. "After you tell me how you got your scar."

"Did you get more Xanax?" Theo asked.

"No." Marisol made a face.

Theo was relieved but also sad.

"I think we should go on the wagon."

Marisol remained silent and then said, "I made a dentist appointment while I was waiting for you."

"You did?"

Marisol nodded.

"Maybe we can still have a double date at the Bellevue Dental Clinic?" Theo said.

They were stalled in traffic, the cabbie's head lost under a cloud of smoke. He honked a few times at a fish truck double-parked in front of them. Theo felt a wave of nausea from the cigarette smoke and air freshener, and she rolled down the window to hang her head over the side. Marisol put her hand on the back of Theo's neck as she puked up a few rounds of nothing.

"Pull over here," Marisol told the cabbie, who was watching Theo in the rearview mirror, disgusted.

Marisol paid him and followed Theo out onto the sidewalk, where she rested on a fire hydrant.

"I hate that guy," she told Theo. "He thinks we're junkies."

"We kind of are."

"Wait here and I'll get you a ginger ale."

Theo lit a cigarette right before Marisol returned with a dusty box of saltine crackers and two ginger ales.

"You're smoking?" she asked Theo incredulously.

"It's actually disgusting," Theo said dropping the cigarette into the gutter.

"Let's go sit in the park and get some fresh air. "

Marisol led them to a bench outside a small, fenced dog park. She took the soda and crackers out of the plastic bag and put them beside Theo. A tall woman with long red hair held her hand up in the air and said, "Touch."

Her dog looked like a miniature golden retriever and leapt high in the air touching her hand with its nose.

"It's like a circus dog," Theo said to Marisol.

Marisol looked up. She took a swig of her ginger ale, watching the dog.

Theo held her ginger ale under her nose and let the fizzing tickle her nostrils.

"Flip," the woman said, making a twirling motion with her hand, and the dog did three backflips in a row.

"Wow," Theo and Marisol said at the same time.

Marisol put two saltine crackers on top of each other.

"Here. I made you dinner," she said, handing the crackers to Theo.

Theo took the crackers and said, "Let's teach Cary Grant to do tricks."

The little dog was now weaving expertly in and out of the owner's legs while she walked.

"I've wasted a lot of my life," Theo said angrily.

Marisol looked at her blankly.

"Do you know after Atlantic City I called to hire you a skywriter?" Theo blurted out.

"What?" Marisol said.

"It doesn't matter. I lost all my money."

Theo lit a new cigarette and said, "I have to quit smoking."

The dog was now jumping through a purple hula hoop.

"Quit smoking if you want to quit smoking," Marisol said, a touch annoyed.

"The skywriter said each letter is the size of the Empire State Building. Do you know that when you see those letters they are ten thousand feet in the air?"

"You're crazy," Marisol said.

"At least I don't have crumbs on my tits."

Marisol looked down and brushed off the cracker crumbs.

"Why you looking at my tits?"

"Because they're perfect."

"Do you know the one night I worked at The Looney Bin Candy grabbed them to see if they were real?"

"What?" Theo said laughing. "Are they?" she asked, reaching for them.

"Come on, Jack," the owner said, leashing up the little dog and leading him out of the park.

"How much does a skywriter cost?" Marisol asked.

"Twelve hundred dollars."

"Are you fucking kidding me?"

"I don't even care about the money," Theo said. " There

are a ton of other factors. Like you would have to be somewhere to see it at the exact right time."

She put her head on Marisol's shoulder and pointed to the sky.

"Like this. And then I would have to have you look up at the right time and the sky would have to be the right blue and the skywriter would have to not be drunk and have good penmanship."

The sky above them was a perfect violet.

"If you could have them write anything, what would have them write?" Marisol asked.

"You have crumbs on your tits."

Marisol punched Theo in the arm.

"No really. It could be right there," Theo said. "Wouldn't you want someone to tell you if you had crumbs on your tits?"

Marisol slid her hand between Theo's thigh and the bench. It was cold out.

"Do you know tomorrow is my birthday?" Theo told Marisol.

"Are you serious?"

Theo nodded.

"How old will you be?"

"Thirty."

"That's a nice age. I'm three years older than you," Marisol said.

Theo traced her finger down a tendon in Marisol's neck.

"Are you hungry?" Theo said.

"Not really, but we should go home and feed Cary Grant."

"Cary Grant," Theo said happily.

But they sat on the bench a little longer, looking at the place in the sky where the skywriter would've been.

Ali Liebegott is the author of the award-winning books *The Beautifully Worthless* and *The IHOP Papers*. In 2010 she took a train trip across America interviewing female poets for a project titled, *The Heart Has Many Doors* — excerpts from these interviews are posted monthly on *The Believer Logger*. In addition, she is the founding editor at Writers Among Artists whose first publication, *Faggot Dinosaur*, was released in 2012. A new edition of *The Beautifully Worthless* was published under the City Lights/Sister Spit imprint in 2013.